THE KELLER FILE
AN AUNT BESSIE COLD CASE MYSTERY
BOOK TEN

DIANA XARISSA

Copyright © 2023 by DX Dunn, LLC

Cover Copyright © 2023 Tell-Tale Book Covers

ISBN: 9798367782004

All rights reserved.

No part of this publication may be reproduced, distributed, or transmitted in any form or by any means, including photocopying, recording, or other electronic or mechanical methods, without the prior written permission of the publisher, except as permitted by U.S. copyright law. For permission requests, contact diana@dianaxarissa.com

The story, all names, characters, and incidents portrayed in this production are fictitious. No identification with actual persons (living or deceased), places, buildings, and products is intended or should be inferred.

First edition 2023

❦ Created with Vellum

CHAPTER 1

"I'm sure Dad's complained about me a lot," Matthew Cheatham said.

Elizabeth Cubbon, known as Bessie to everyone, shook her head. "Not at all. He doesn't talk about his family very often." She wasn't lying. Andrew didn't tell her much about his family, although she had heard a few things about Matthew.

"He'd be justified in complaining about me, really," Matthew told her with a sigh. "I should be old enough to take care of myself, but here I am, staying with my father so he can look after me."

"I was under the impression that you were here to look after your father."

Matthew laughed. "Yes, okay, we're looking after each other." He sighed again and then waved a hand at the sea in front of them. "He thinks that being by the water will be therapeutic."

"I agree. I credit the sea air and my daily beach walks with keeping me fit and healthy."

"And if you don't mind me saying so, you've lived a long time."

Bessie bristled. "I'm in the later stage of middle age, but I certainly wouldn't say that I've lived a long time."

"Later stage of…." Matthew trailed off and then smiled. "I hope I can continue to be as healthy and vibrant as you are as I get older."

The pair fell silent for a moment as they sat side by side on the rock behind Bessie's cottage on Laxey Beach.

"I should be grateful that my father brought me along on his holiday, really, shouldn't I?" Matthew asked eventually.

"I believe he isn't meant to be travelling on his own at the moment."

"But he usually brings Helen. I love my sister dearly, but I wouldn't want to stay in a cottage on the beach with her for a fortnight."

"I think Helen is lovely."

Matthew nodded. "She is lovely, but she never cared for my second wife, and I can almost hear her thinking 'I told you so' whenever I say anything about my divorce."

"That must be difficult."

"It is. Dad didn't care for my second wife, either, by the time we separated, but he was very supportive when we first began seeing one another. But I promised myself I wasn't going to talk about her or about my divorce. Tell me your life story instead."

What is keeping Andrew? Bessie wondered, glancing up the beach towards the holiday cottage where he and Matthew were staying. "I'm afraid I've led a rather dull life," she said.

"My father said that you've lived in your cottage for a really long time."

"I bought it when I was eighteen, and it's been my home ever since. I can't imagine living anywhere else."

"Eighteen? I didn't have ten pounds to my name when I was eighteen, let alone enough money to buy a house."

Bessie nodded. "I inherited a small sum, enough to allow me to purchase the cottage. Houses on the island were considerably less expensive in those days, of course. And my cottage was quite a bit smaller as well. I've added two extensions in the years since I bought it."

"So you grew up on the island?"

"Actually, no, I grew up in Cleveland, Ohio, in the United States."

Matthew stared at her. "Really? Then how did you end up owning a cottage on the beach on the Isle of Man?"

Bessie glanced behind them again, but there was no sign of Andrew anywhere. "I'll give you the short version," she said with a chuckle. "I was born on the island, but, when I was two, my parents decided to emigrate to the US. We moved to Ohio, where some of our family was already settled. We were there for fifteen years before my parents decided to return to the island."

"When you were seventeen?"

"Yes, when I was seventeen. My older sister, who was nineteen, stayed behind. She and the young man she'd been seeing for over a year got married very quickly. My parents refused to allow me to remain with her or to marry the young man I'd been seeing."

"I would have been furious."

Bessie laughed. "I was very angry. They practically had to drag me on to the ship for the journey back to the island. I spent the entire sailing sobbing in our cabin. I thought my heart was broken and that I'd never get over losing Matthew."

"His name was Matthew?"

"It was, Matthew Saunders."

"Did you call him Matt?"

Bessie shook her head. "We hadn't been seeing one another for very long, really. I was still referring to him as Mr. Saunders most of the time. I'd dared to use his Christian name only once or twice. We were much more formal in those days, of course."

"Everyone calls me Matt. Matthew feels formal to me. But I interrupted. You cried all the way back to the island. How did you go from that to owning your cottage?"

"We'd been back on the island for only a short while when I received a letter from Matthew. He'd decided he couldn't live without me, so he was coming to get me. I was almost deliriously happy for the next few weeks as I waited for his arrival."

"I'm sorry. I can tell this isn't going to end well. You don't have to tell me anything else."

Bessie shook her head. "Everyone on the island knows the story. I don't mind telling it, really, although it's still painful, even though many years have passed."

Matt patted her arm. "I should have had my father tell me about his friends on the island, shouldn't I? Then I wouldn't have had to ask awkward questions. I've been rather self-absorbed lately, and it never occurred to me to ask him about the people I'm going to meet while I'm here."

"I'm certain he'll be happy to tell you about everyone he knows here. But let me finish my story. Matthew didn't survive the voyage. He passed away just a few days before his ship was due to dock in Liverpool. Before he'd left the US, he'd written his will and, in it, he left all of his possessions to me. His parents were kind enough to sell his things and send me the money. It wasn't a great deal of money, but it was enough to allow me to purchase my cottage, which was essential because I blamed my parents for Matthew's death and couldn't bear living with them any longer."

"I'm so sorry," Matt said. "Your parents must have felt terrible, too."

Bessie frowned. "They may have. They probably did, actually, but I was too angry to care how they felt. I regret it now, but after Matthew's death, I never spoke to them again."

Matt was silent for a moment. "And you've lived on your own ever since?" he asked eventually.

"I have. There was another man who once proposed to me years ago, but he lived in Australia, and I found that I loved the island too much to agree to leave. I can't imagine how different my life would have been if I'd married him and moved halfway around the world."

"I've been to Australia. It's beautiful and the weather is amazing, but I wouldn't want to live there."

"No one could complain about the weather here today."

Matt looked up at the cloudless sky and nodded. "Summers in England are usually very nice. It gets a good deal hotter in Australia."

"All the more reason to be glad I stayed here."

"Don't you get lonely, though?" Matt sighed. "Sorry, that's probably a rude question. I'm just struggling a bit. I'm living on my own for the first time in a long time, and I find myself just wandering around my flat, feeling lonely."

"I quite enjoy being on my own. I suppose, over the years, I've become quite accustomed to my own company. I can't imagine sharing my cottage with anyone, really, and I also can't imagine living anywhere else."

"Maybe if I give it some time I'll come to enjoy living alone. There are some advantages. I get to eat what I want and watch whatever I want on the telly, but I'm not very good at looking after myself. I tend to eat too much rubbish and watch too much football."

"I don't even have a television."

Matt stared at her. "What do you do all day?"

Bessie laughed. "I read a great deal. I'm also something of an amateur historian. I work with the librarian at the Manx Museum on various different projects. At the moment, she's having me catalogue several boxes of old papers, most of which haven't seen the light of day in a very long time."

"That sounds interesting, but surely after a long day of cataloguing, you'd enjoy watching a sitcom, or maybe a drama."

"Maybe, but you don't miss what you've never had. Buying my cottage took nearly every penny that Matthew had left me. My advocate invested what was left on my behalf. I've been fortunate enough to have been able to live ever since on the income that those investments generated, but for many years I had to be very frugal. By the time I felt that I could afford to buy a television, I'd found other ways to fill my time."

"What sort of books do you read?"

"Mostly murder mysteries, although I'll read just about anything if I'm desperate. In the days when I first moved into my cottage and money was very tight, I used to borrow most of my books from friends, and I'd read whatever they were willing to lend me. I visited the library in Douglas as often as I could, but it was a bus journey away and I didn't always have bus fare."

"I suppose you didn't have a car."

"I've never owned a car. I never learned to drive. For many years, I relied on the island's buses and trains, but when a friend of mine opened a small taxi company in Laxey, his service was a good deal more convenient. Because we were friends, he gave me special rates, and by that time my investments had grown to the point where I could afford to indulge in taxis rather than buses for most journeys."

"And you aren't tempted to learn to drive now?"

Bessie laughed. "I do think about it from time to time.

My friend sold his company to a large Douglas-based one. They still give me a substantial discount, but I've not always been fond of all of their drivers. Having never even attempted it, the idea of driving a car is quite terrifying, though."

"I can teach you to drive while I'm here. I taught my kids. You can't be any worse than they were."

"It's a tempting offer, but I think I'll stick to taxis and friends."

"You know where to find me if you change your mind."

Bessie nodded. "You brought your car with you, didn't you?"

"Dad flew over, but I came on the ferry with my car. I'm not fond of flying, and I'm even less fond of hire cars." He glanced over his shoulder at the car that was parked in the small parking area outside of Bessie's cottage. "And I'm very, very, very fond of my car."

Bessie looked over at it and shrugged. "I'm afraid cars all look rather alike to me."

"I won't bore you with any of the details, but believe me when I say that she's something special."

"At least you won't be stuck in the cottage when your father is busy elsewhere."

"Exactly. Dad has his hire car and I have my own car. We can both come and go as we please."

Bessie looked back up the beach. *What is keeping Andrew?* she wondered. She didn't mind chatting with Matt, but she'd much rather have Andrew there to help keep the conversation flowing.

"So, tell me about the other people who will be at dinner tonight," Matt said after a minute. "Dad told me that he's invited all of his friends from the island so that they can all meet me."

"I believe everyone from the unit has been invited, along

with a few other special guests. Your father has reserved a private dining room at the Seaview for us."

"I've heard the Seaview is gorgeous. Helen said she wants to stay there one day."

"It's the nicest hotel on the island, and the restaurant does wonderful food."

"I hope you don't think I'm being nosy, but I'd love to hear a bit about the people I'll be meeting later. It's difficult being the only new person in a group of people who've known one another for years."

Bessie nodded. "I understand."

"Dad told me that I'd be meeting John, Donna, and someone else, a young police constable, but I've forgotten his name already. I'd be grateful if you could tell me about each of them, especially the constable's name," Matt said with a sheepish grin.

"The constable is Hugh Watterson," Bessie said with a laugh. "He'll be the young man who looks no more than fifteen, even though he'll be at the dinner with his wife and daughter."

"Hugh Watterson – got it. I'm afraid if you tell me what his wife and daughter are called, I'll forget."

"His wife is Grace and his daughter is Aalish, which is the Manx form of Alice."

"What a lovely name. I don't think I'll forget that. Am I remembering correctly that Hugh is in school at the moment?"

"He's gone back to school to earn a degree. He's doing everything he can to advance his career now that he's married with a family."

"How old is Aalish?"

"She'll be two in December. Grace is expecting again. She's due in February."

"What an exciting time for all of them. I hope they have

lots of extra help around. In my experience, grandparents are excellent at helping out."

Bessie nodded. "Both sets of grandparents are very involved."

"What about Donna, then?"

"It's not Donna, it's Doona, which is another Manx name."

"Thank goodness I asked! I'd hate to get it wrong. Doona, right, I'm going to remember that. Tell me about Doona."

Bessie grinned. "Doona Moore is somewhere in her forties. We met in a Manx language class, years ago now. She was working towards ending her second marriage and she'd moved to Laxey for a complete change of scenery. I believe she was hoping to meet other people around her age in the class, but she was the only person under the age of sixty taking the class."

Matt laughed. "I have a friend who did that same thing once. He signed up to take a class, hoping to meet women, but the entire class was just other men who'd all signed up for the same reason. He dropped out after the first session."

"Luckily for me, Doona stayed, and, over time, we've become very close friends. She used to work for the Laxey Constabulary at the reception desk, but she quit working after an unexpected inheritance."

"How very fortunate for her."

"I'm not certain she'd put it that way. It was her second husband who passed away. They were separated, but not divorced, when he died."

Matt frowned. "That sounds vaguely familiar. Is his murder the one that my father got involved in at the holiday park in the Lake District a few years ago?"

Bessie nodded. "That was where your father and I met. He was staying in the cabin next door to the one that Doona and I were sharing. Doona was a suspect in her husband's murder, and your father was kind enough to help us get through the investigation."

"And then Doona inherited something from the dead man?"

"He'd never rewritten his will after he and Doona separated. I believe he continued to hope that they might be reunited one day. Doona inherited his entire estate, which was substantial."

"Did my father tell me something about him owning part of the holiday park?"

"He did own part of the holiday park, and now Doona owns his share and spends a great deal of her time managing it from a distance."

"That sounds difficult."

"It is difficult. Obviously, summer is their busiest season. She actually went across in July to help out and returned to the island only yesterday. I'm looking forward to seeing her later."

Bessie turned her head and looked up the beach again. While she was enjoying her conversation with Matt, she'd prefer it if Andrew joined them sooner rather than later.

"That just leaves John. I believe he's an inspector with the local constabulary."

"He is. Inspector John Rockwell is also in his forties. He and Doona have been involved with one another for some time now."

"Good for them. I assume from the name that Doona is from the island. Is John?"

"No, he moved to the island from Manchester. He and his wife were hoping for better opportunities for their children."

Matt frowned. "I think I missed something. He has a wife? I assume she's an ex-wife, if he's involved with Doona now."

"Sorry, I didn't mean to confuse you. When John first

moved to the island, he brought his wife, Sue, and their two children, Thomas and Amy, with him. Sue hated the island, though, so after a year she returned to Manchester with Thomas and Amy."

"That must be tough for John. How old are the kids?"

"It was difficult for John. Thomas and Amy are teenagers, and he missed them terribly when they were in Manchester. Fortunately, they weren't there for long."

"Oh? Did they decide they wanted to live with John instead?"

"No." Bessie sighed. "I don't know why I'm hesitating. Everyone on the island knows the story."

"You don't have to tell me anything. I can always ask Dad to fill me in."

Bessie laughed. "And, of course, your father knows the story, too. Basically, Sue very quickly remarried. She'd never stopped loving one of her former boyfriends, and they'd crossed paths again when he began treating her mother for cancer during the year that Sue was living on the island."

"He was treating her on the island?"

Bessie shook her head. "I'm telling this badly. He was in Manchester, and so was Sue's mother. Sue kept flying back and forth to be with her mother for treatments. Then she was reunited with Harvey and, well, they rekindled their romance."

"And when she remarried, she sent the children to live with John?"

"No, when she remarried, she and Harvey headed to Africa for a lengthy honeymoon. He'd always dreamed of using his skills in a developing country where he felt he could make a real difference. Sadly, at some point during their travels, Sue fell ill and never recovered."

"Those poor children."

Bessie nodded. "It's been difficult for them and for John,

but Doona does what she can to help. From what I've seen, they're both great kids. They've been invited to tonight's dinner, too."

"I'm looking forward to meeting them. Is there anything else I should know about John or Doona or Hugh or their families?"

Bessie thought for a minute. "I don't think so. I've given you the basics, anyway."

"And that's everyone who will be at dinner tonight?"

"That's everyone from the island who will be there. The others from the cold case unit will be there, too, though."

Matt stared at her for a minute. "Others from the cold case unit? You said 'unit' earlier, but I didn't really think about what you meant. What cold case unit is this, then?"

CHAPTER 2

Bessie frowned. Now that everyone on the island knew about the cold case unit, thanks to Dan Ross's article in the *Isle of Man Times*, it had never occurred to her that Andrew's son might not. She took a deep breath, stalling for time while she tried to think.

"Dad isn't just coming over here for regular holidays, then, is he?" Matt asked.

"No, he's not. Several months ago, he started a cold case unit that meets here on a monthly basis. We've been considering cases from all over the world."

Matt sighed. "I have been far too caught up in my own drama lately. I should have suspected that there was more to these monthly trips to the island than just a desire for sea air."

Bessie laughed. "Your father does appreciate the sea air."

"Let's back up the conversation a bit, then. Who, of the people we've discussed, is part of the cold case unit?"

"Hugh, Doona, and John. And me, of course."

"So it's a very nontraditional cold case unit."

"It is, yes. Your father has mentioned having to work

quite hard to get permission to put it together in the way that he wanted."

"And who else is part of the unit?"

"Two retired inspectors from Scotland Yard. Charles Morris and Harry Blake."

"Both names are vaguely familiar. I suspect I've met them both at least once or twice."

"Your sister knew them both before she started travelling to the island with your father."

Matt chuckled. "But Helen has always been more involved in Dad's life than I am. If Dad's known them for years, then they were probably in and out of the house while I was growing up, but I was at home as little as possible until I went away to uni."

Bessie wasn't certain how to reply to that. "I'm sorry," she said eventually.

Matt looked surprised. "Oh, it wasn't because life at home was bad or anything. I loved my parents and tolerated my siblings, but my closest friend lived just across the road. He was an only child with two working parents, so, when I went there, we had the entire house to ourselves. We used to spend hours watching telly and eating everything in their kitchen. I spent most weekends over there, too. Victor and I were pretty much inseparable."

"Are you still friends now?" Bessie had to ask.

"We are, actually. We went to the same uni and lived together for many years after that. I finally moved out of our shared flat when I got married for the first time. He got married a few years later, and our wives got to be close friends, too. Obviously, we don't see each other all that often now. He moved to Brighton about twenty years ago. As far as I'm concerned, though, he's still my closest friend."

"How nice for you."

"It's great, but it did mean that I didn't spend much time

THE KELLER FILE

at home when I was younger. If I did meet either of the two men you named, I've forgotten everything about them. Tell me what I need to know before I meet them later, please."

"Harry was a homicide inspector. As I said, he's retired now. That's really all that I know about him."

Matt laughed. "That doesn't surprise me. Members of the police can be notoriously tight-lipped about their private lives."

"I suppose I can understand why."

"Oh, yes, of course. So that's Harry. What about Charles?"

"Charles worked in Missing Persons. I understand that he's something of an expert in the field. He often works as a consultant on cases around the world."

"That may be why the name is familiar to me, actually. I'm fairly certain he was part of the team that investigated the disappearance of that model who vanished in London a few years ago."

"He may well have been."

"She disappeared from the street just one over from where I live. As a consequence, I followed the case quite closely."

"I followed it quite closely, too, as the woman in question had been born on the island. I was very relieved when she turned up unharmed."

Matt nodded. "Her reappearance was almost as dramatic as her disappearance had been. I still think she did it all herself for publicity."

Bessie shrugged. "I doubt anyone will ever know the full story there."

"And they're both going to be at the dinner tonight?"

"Yes, they are, or rather, I know they've both been invited. I haven't had a chance to speak to your father about the plans, though. One or both of them might not be able to attend for some reason."

"We'll have to ask Dad about them when he gets here. I wonder what's keeping him."

"I've been wondering the same thing. I hope nothing is wrong." Bessie looked up the beach at the cottage in which Andrew always stayed when he visited the island.

"Maybe I'd better go and see…" Matt began. He trailed off as the cottage's sliding door opened and Andrew stepped outside.

"I am so sorry," Andrew said when he reached them. "I never intended to abandon you both in that way."

Bessie laughed. "We've been having a lovely chat, although I may have said things I shouldn't have, as I told him about the cold case unit."

Andrew shrugged. "It's definitely not a secret any longer. Now that Dan Ross has written about it, reporters from around the world have been ringing up and asking me to speak to them about our work. I've turned them all down so far, but I may have to agree to do something eventually."

"I told Bessie that I should have suspected that you weren't just coming to the island every month for a holiday."

"I would, though," Andrew replied as he looked up and down the beach. "It's a lovely island, and I'm seriously considering buying a house here."

"Really? I didn't know that," Matt said.

"I'm spending a fortnight here every month. While I love staying right on Laxey Beach, it might be nicer to have my own home here. I could leave some of my things behind and not have to bring two large suitcases every time I visit, for a start."

Matt nodded. "That makes sense. Have you started looking at properties yet?"

"I looked at a few some months ago, but then there was a fire and the subsequent police investigation, and I put the whole idea to one side. Now, though, it's summer and the beach is full of visitors, and I'm starting to think that I'd be a lot happier somewhere a bit quieter."

As a ball suddenly bounced past them, with two teenaged boys in hot pursuit, Matt laughed.

"I can see your point," he said.

"Charles and Harry are both staying on the beach, too," Andrew told him. "Did Bessie tell you about them?"

"She did. She said they were former colleagues of yours, so I probably met them when I was younger."

"I'm sure you did, although I've no idea when or where. They typically stay at the Seaview, but this is the hotel's busiest season, and they were unable to accommodate Charles and Harry during the summer months. We've already booked their rooms for next summer, though, so this should be their last month in the holiday cottages."

"I thought they both appreciated the extra room the cottages give them," Bessie said.

"They do, but, on balance, they both agreed that they'd rather have room service and the ability to walk to our meetings," Andrew told her.

"That would be nice," Bessie agreed.

"You meet at the Seaview?" Matt asked.

"Usually. We have been known to meet in one of the holiday cottages or even at Bessie's, but the Seaview has large, comfortable conference rooms, and they provide catering as well."

"I'm not going to be allowed to attend the meetings, am I?"

"Sorry, but the meetings are limited to approved unit members only. The cases we discuss are all confidential," Andrew replied.

"How many cases have you considered so far?"

"Ten," Andrew said.

"And have you been able to help solve any of them?"

"We've managed to solve them all," Andrew said. "But you mustn't repeat that. We don't officially release information about our success rate."

"Congratulations. That's really amazing. At least, it sounds amazing to me," Matt said.

"It is pretty amazing," Andrew agreed. "When we started, I had hopes of solving one case in every ten we considered. We've had much more success than we really should be having."

"Why?" Matt asked.

Andrew shrugged. "If I knew the answer to that, I'd be shouting it from the rooftops so that policing agencies across the world could duplicate our success."

"It is a very unconventional cold case unit."

"It is, and over the past year or so I've spoken to several other people who've been working on setting up similar units. I've encouraged all of them to try different things. Clearly, an unconventional approach can be useful."

"I do hope you weren't delayed because something was wrong," Bessie said.

"Not at all. I needed to ring the inspector who is in charge of the case that we are going to be looking at this month. We had a quick conversation, and I was on my way out here when my estate agent rang."

Matt laughed. "And they never want to ring off once they've reached you."

"He'd sent me the particulars for over a dozen properties, and he really wanted to talk about each and every one of them. He said the more I told him what I liked and disliked about each of them, the better he'd get at finding my perfect home."

"I do hope you aren't expecting to find the perfect place," Bessie said. "The island has limited inventory, and prices are rising all the time. If you really do want to buy a house here, you may have to compromise on some of your wish list, and you may have to move quickly."

"That's more or less what the estate agent said," Andrew replied with a sigh. "I didn't care for any of the properties that he'd sent, but, in the end, I've agreed to take a look at a few of them."

"Today?" Matt asked.

Andrew shook his head. "First thing tomorrow morning. I need to be at the first property at eight. We're going to go from there."

"Do you want me to come along with you?" Bessie asked. "And before that, do you want me to look at the listings and tell you everything I know about the houses?"

"Yes and yes," Andrew replied. "Although there aren't many properties for sale at the moment. These properties are all in Douglas, so you may know less about them than you did when I was looking at options closer to Laxey."

"I can always ring a friend or two in Douglas if you have questions that I can't answer. For now, though, I'm curious to see the listings."

"I am, too," Matt said. "It will be interesting to compare what's available on the island to the properties I've been looking at lately."

"You've been looking at mostly flats, though," Andrew said. "My listings are almost all for small, detached houses."

"I'm still curious. I probably wouldn't be able to find a job over here, even if I wanted to move, but sitting here, in the glorious sunshine, it's quite tempting to look," Matt said.

"Do you want me to bring the listing paperwork down here, then?" Andrew asked.

Bessie shook her head. "As much as I love the sunshine, I've had enough for now. I'm ready for a cup of tea and a biscuit, I believe."

"Oh, well, if there are biscuits on offer," Matt said with a chuckle.

"Come over to my cottage," Bessie invited them. "I'll make tea and we can look at the listings together."

Andrew went back to his cottage to get the paperwork while Bessie and Matt walked to Bessie's cottage.

"What can I do to help?" Matt asked as Bessie opened her door.

"Just sit at the kitchen table and relax," she replied. "Making tea isn't a difficult job, and you've no idea where to find anything, anyway."

Andrew knocked a few minutes later. Once they were all settled around the table with tea and biscuits in front of them, he handed Bessie a large envelope.

"That's everything that the agent sent me. I've marked the ones that I'm going to see tomorrow."

Bessie pulled the pages of listings out of the envelope. "What did you ask him to find you?"

"I told him I needed at least two bedrooms and would prefer two bathrooms as well. I also asked to be as close to the centre of Douglas as possible," Andrew replied.

Bessie looked at the first listing. "This one is in Onchan, and on the outskirts of Onchan at that."

Andrew sighed. "Is that one of the ones I'm going to see?"

"I don't see any notes on it," Bessie replied, handing him the paper.

"Ah, no, I ruled this one out because it has only a single bathroom, and it is on the ground floor. The bedrooms are on the first floor, and I'm not prepared to rush up and down stairs in the middle of the night."

"Neither am I, and I'm quite a bit younger," Matt said as Andrew passed him the listing. "Is that the correct price, though? I wasn't expecting houses on the island to be that expensive."

"They've gone up very rapidly in the past few years," Bessie told him. "The government has lowered taxes on both people and companies, so a great many banks and insurance companies have established offices here. That's brought in a large number of their staff who've been relocated here from elsewhere."

"And that's driven up prices," Matt concluded.

"Indeed," Bessie replied before she turned her attention to the next listing.

"This one is in a new housing estate on the very edge of Douglas," she told Andrew. "I suppose there are some advantages to buying something new, but the location won't be terribly convenient."

"I wasn't planning on seeing that one, either," Andrew told her. "It doesn't seem to have any character."

"New houses often don't," Matt said. "No doubt the estate agent will tell you that the house is a blank slate, ready for you to give it character, but I'd rather buy something a bit more interesting."

Bessie looked around her cosy cottage. It definitely had character, at least in her eyes.

The next three properties were all similar, newly constructed homes in the new housing estates that were popping up all around Douglas. Andrew wasn't planning on seeing any of them. Bessie was happy to turn to the sixth property and see something different.

"This one is quite close to the Manx Museum," she told Andrew.

He nodded. "It's a great location, on the hill above the town centre, but it's in a terrace, and it needs a lot of work."

Bessie looked at the pictures and then squinted at one of them. "Is that water damage?"

"I'm not certain, but I thought it might be," Andrew

replied. "I got the feeling that the pictures were all very carefully taken to show the property in the very best light."

"Surely that's to be expected with estate agents," Matt said.

"Yes, but some of these have been taken at very odd angles," Andrew said as Bessie handed Matt the listing.

He looked at the pictures and then nodded. "I see what you mean. Why would you take a picture of just part of the kitchen? Especially as the rest of the picture is of a blank wall."

"I hope you aren't going to see that one," Bessie said.

"I was tempted, actually, just to see what they're trying to hide, but in the end, I decided it wasn't worth my time. The last four are the ones I'm going to see."

"This looks to be a lovely little cottage," Bessie said as she looked at the next sheet. "It's not near the centre of Douglas, but if you don't mind that, it appears to have been well looked after."

Andrew nodded. "That's the first property on my list for tomorrow. The rooms are small, but probably not much smaller than the rooms in the holiday cottage. It isn't an ideal location, but it's a good price."

"I thought you said you weren't looking at flats," Bessie said as she turned to the next property.

"I told the estate agent I wasn't interested in flats, but he threw that one in, just to give me an idea of what I could afford if I were willing to consider a flat."

"To be fair, a flat would be a lot less work for you," Matt said. "If you buy a detached house, you'll have a garden to tend, which won't be easy if you're on the island for only two weeks at a time."

"And that's why I'm going to take a look at that flat. It's right on the promenade, so I could easily walk to the shops and restaurants, and it has sea views," Andrew replied.

"It does look as if it's in good condition," Bessie said after she'd looked at the pictures on the listing.

"They converted the building into flats a few years ago, so everything inside the flat is fairly new," Andrew told her.

Bessie handed the sheet to Matt and then looked at the next property. "This looks lovely, but it's very dear."

Andrew nodded. "It's outside my budget, but the estate agent convinced me to go and have a look at it anyway. He insisted that prices are always negotiable, and it is a lovely little house."

"It looks as if the current owners have poured a lot of money into it," Bessie said. "The kitchen is fabulous."

"Help me remember not to fall in love with it," Andrew replied. "I really don't want to spend that much money on a holiday home."

"That is a lot of money," Matt said. "But I can see why. The kitchen is quite wonderful, isn't it? Of course, Dad doesn't do all that much cooking. It would be wasted on him."

Bessie laughed and then turned her attention to the last property in the pile. She read the listing carefully and then read it again.

"What's wrong?" Andrew asked. "You've gone very quiet."

Bessie shook her head. "I'm confused by this listing."

"Why? It seems straightforward enough. I'm really excited to see that property, actually. It appears to be almost exactly what I want. Obviously, I'd rather it was in Laxey or Lonan, but it's a lovely Victorian terraced house with three bedrooms and two bathrooms, within walking distance of the shops."

"I thought you wanted a detached house," Matt said.

Andrew shrugged. "I'm prepared to consider anything. There aren't many detached properties near the centre of

Douglas – not in my budget, anyway. And this one looks quite special."

Bessie nodded. "It is quite special. I know the owner. I'm just shocked that it's on the market. I had no idea that Hazel was planning to sell her beloved family home."

CHAPTER 3

Andrew frowned. "Is this Hazel a close friend?"

"Not very close, but I would have thought that I'd have heard if she'd decided to put her house on the market. She loves that house."

"Maybe you should tell me all about Hazel," Andrew suggested.

Bessie nodded and then shook her head. "I will, but first I'm going to ring her." She checked her address book and was happy to discover that she'd remembered her friend's phone number correctly. She dialled the number and then waited anxiously for Hazel to answer.

"You're frowning," Andrew said as Bessie put the receiver down.

"The number is no longer in service," she said, feeling confused.

"Do you want to ring someone else or tell me about her first?"

"I'm going to ring a mutual friend. She should know what's happening."

Bessie checked her address book again and then dialled

another number. "Esther, it's Bessie Cubbon," she told the answering machine when it answered. "Please ring me back when you have a moment. I'm a bit concerned about Hazel."

She put the receiver down and frowned at Andrew. "I could ring some others, but it's probably best to wait and see what Esther has to say."

"Tell me about Hazel, then," Andrew requested.

Bessie nodded and then took a sip of her tea. "I'm sorry, but my mind is all over the place. I don't even know where to start."

"How long have you known her?"

"A very long time. She used to live in one of the cottages further down the beach from here, many years ago. Her parents owned it, and she was still living at home when I bought my cottage. She's a few years older than I am, and when I first moved in, she was delighted to have a neighbour close to her age."

"So you became friends," Andrew said when Bessie paused.

"We did, although I'm certain that I was a disappointment to her. She was hoping for someone with whom to go shopping and out for meals and whatnot, but I was in mourning and didn't really want to go out at all. We used to walk on the beach together, though, sometimes for hours on end. She was incredibly bored at home and rather desperate to find herself a husband."

Matt laughed. "The poor girl."

"That was what young women did in those days," Bessie replied. "That was another reason why she was excited to have me as a neighbour. I was a young woman living on my own, which simply wasn't done back then. Her parents didn't actually approve of our friendship at first. They were concerned that I'd be a bad influence on Hazel."

"I assume they changed their minds once they got to know you," Andrew said.

Bessie nodded. "I got to know them quite well over the years. They were especially kind to me during that difficult first year."

"What happened after the first year?" Matt asked after a moment.

"I'm sorry. I'm not telling the story very well. After a year or so, Hazel finally found herself a husband. Otto was twelve years older than Hazel, and he'd been widowed some years before he'd moved to the island. He and Hazel went out for about three months before he proposed. As soon as they were married, they bought a house in Douglas."

"This house?" Andrew asked, holding up the listing.

Bessie nodded. "That house. I can still remember Hazel telling me all about it after the first time they'd toured it. It was much larger than the cottage that she shared with her parents, and she and Otto were the only ones who were going to live there. They'd have so much space they'd never fill it all."

"Why do I doubt that?" Andrew murmured. "Things have a way of accumulating and filling every available space."

"A year later, Hazel fell pregnant. Otto was surprised and perhaps not very happy about it. He and his first wife had never had children, and Hazel told me that he'd believed that he was unable to have them."

"Based on what?" Andrew wondered.

Bessie shrugged. "Hazel said something about him having had some sort of fever as a child. After he'd recovered, the doctors apparently told him that he'd never be able to have children."

"Did he suspect Hazel of cheating, then?" Matt asked.

"He did. Apparently, they had a huge fight, and she moved back in with her parents for several months. We walked on the beach every day while she was here. Eventually, she had the baby, and he looked so much like Otto that even he had to admit that his doctors might have been wrong."

"Of course, there wasn't any DNA testing back then," Matt said. "What about blood types?"

"I assume they were compatible, but I don't really know. I just remember how happy Hazel was when she and Otto were reunited. While they'd been apart, she'd really come to rely on her parents, though, so once she moved back to Douglas, she persuaded Otto to let her parents move in with them."

"And that huge house suddenly felt very small indeed," Andrew suggested.

"Very likely, but they all seemed happy with the new arrangement. Hazel's parents put their cottage on the market a few months later and it sold very quickly. After that, I rarely saw Hazel."

Andrew pulled out a notebook and jotted a few things in it. "Hazel and Otto had only one child?" he asked.

"No, they had two. Hazel gave birth to a second boy about two years after the first. The boys are Patrick and Paul, but I forget which is the older of the two."

Andrew made another note. "And is Otto still alive?"

"No, he passed away some years ago," Bessie replied, trying to remember the details. "Hazel's parents died within six months of one another in the early seventies. If I'm correct, Otto passed away not much more than a year later."

"Leaving poor Hazel on her own with the children," Matt said.

"The children were already in their thirties or forties," Bessie told him. "Patrick must have already been married, with children of his own. Paul never married. He lived his entire life with a dear friend, James, whom he'd met at uni.

They died together in a terrible car accident about ten years ago."

"Where is Patrick now?" Andrew asked.

"I believe he's living in a care home in Douglas," Bessie said. "His wife, Margaret, passed away when their children were still fairly young. They had two girls."

Andrew looked up from his notebook. "Tell me about the girls, then."

"This isn't a criminal investigation," Bessie said.

"But it could be," Andrew countered.

"And Dad always has to get all of the information he can about everyone," Matt told her. "His notebooks must be full of information that he's never needed to know about people who only crossed his path once or twice in his life."

Andrew laughed. "I'm sorry. I don't have to know everything about Hazel and her family, but you seemed very concerned about her and the fact that her house is for sale. I suppose I could have been a bit more subtle in asking about her, though, and maybe made my notes later, when you weren't around."

Bessie shook her head. "Don't apologise. You're trying to help, and I truly appreciate it. It just feels odd talking about my friend in this way."

"We don't have to finish," Andrew said.

"But we should," Bessie replied firmly. "As you say, it might be a criminal investigation. Where was I? Patrick and his wife had two daughters, Laura and Delores. They must be in their fifties by now. The last I knew, Laura had moved across. She trained as a teacher, and after teaching on the island for several years, she took a job in Liverpool. The last time I spoke to Hazel, she told me that Laura had since moved to Leeds." She stopped and waited while Andrew took his notes.

"I don't have Hazel's surname," he said when he looked up.

"She's Hazel Lace," Bessie replied. "She was Hazel Cannell before she got married."

"So Otto was Otto Lace?" Andrew checked.

"Yes, and the boys had the same surname, too. Laura is still Laura Lace, or she was the last I knew. Delores is back to using Lace, or so I believe."

"Back to using Lace?" Andrew repeated.

"Delores has been married three or four times," Bessie explained. "Hazel told me once that Delores had decided to go back to using Lace as her surname after her second divorce. Hazel said it had simplified things after her other marriage, or marriages, fell apart."

"And is Delores still on the island?" Andrew asked.

Bessie nodded. "She was the last time I spoke to Hazel."

"And when was that?" was the next question.

Bessie sighed. "I'm going to have to think for a moment." She shut her eyes and sat back in her chair. "I should have made a point of ringing her more regularly, but we typically spoke only on odd occasions," Bessie said eventually. "I definitely spoke to her around Christmas. She rang me to wish me a Merry Christmas because she hadn't bothered to send cards this year."

"I don't think many people are sending Christmas cards any longer," Matt said.

"I still send them," Bessie told him. "And, in this instance, it's good that I did, because that was what made Hazel ring me. We had a lovely long chat, and I got to hear all about Patrick and Laura and Delores. Sadly, I don't believe I've spoken to her since, though."

Andrew made another note. "Is there anyone else you can ring to check on Hazel?" he asked when he looked up.

Bessie flipped through her address book. "I can try one or

two others. The one person I'm certain would know, other than Esther, passed away last year, sadly." She went through the book again and then dialled a number.

"Agnes? It's Bessie. How are you?"

"Bessie? Bessie who?"

"Bessie Cubbon, up in Laxey."

"Laxey? I don't know anyone in Laxey," the woman replied before she put the phone down firmly.

Bessie stared at her receiver and then sighed. "I believe Agnes is having trouble with her memory," she said.

"We can wait and see what Esther has to say," Andrew said. "It's nearly time to head to Ramsey, anyway."

Bessie glanced at the clock and then nodded. "I need to change into something more appropriate for a nice dinner at the island's fanciest hotel."

"Oh dear. I might not have brought anything appropriate," Matt said.

"You can borrow a shirt from my suitcase," Andrew told him. "You'll be fine."

The pair left Bessie so that she could get ready. It didn't take her long to change and brush her short grey bob into place. A coat of lipstick and a pat of powder was as much makeup as she ever wore. She was pacing back and forth in her kitchen when her phone rang.

"Hello?"

"Bessie? It's Esther."

"Hello. How are you?"

Esther laughed. "How long do you have? I can give you the long answer or the short answer."

"I'm afraid I'm going to have to ask for the short answer. I'm supposed to be going out for dinner in just a few minutes."

"I'm being treated for five different problems, some of them to do with age. My doctor reckons that if the treat ments don't kill me, I'll outlive him. He's thirty-five, and I'm fighting to stay alive only because he's so handsome."

Bessie laughed. "I'm sorry you're poorly, but it sounds as if you're staying positive about it."

"I don't have a choice. If I worry too much, I'll worry myself into an early grave. Although, to be fair, at my age it won't be too early, will it?"

"I promise that I'll ring you back tomorrow so that I can hear all about everything that you're going through, but for tonight, I was hoping you could tell me what's going on with Hazel."

"That's what you said in your message, so I rang Hazel before I rang you to see if there was something wrong. Her number is out of service."

"Yes, I know. That was why I rang you. I rang Hazel because a friend of mine is looking for a house and was sent the particulars for Hazel's property."

"Are you quite certain it's Hazel's house? Maybe it's another house in the terrace. They all look very similar from the outside."

"The address matches, but besides that, there are pictures of the interior. You'll never persuade me that anyone else on the island has that wallpaper in their spare bedroom."

Esther laughed. "It is rather awful, isn't it? I don't know what Hazel was thinking. I've always wanted to ask her about it, but I've never been brave enough to actually do so."

"I'm not as polite as you are. I did ask her. Apparently, the wallpaper was a gift from Otto's mother. Hazel met her only a few times, but when she and Otto bought the house, his mother sent over a huge box of items that she said were to help them make their house a home. Do you remember the lamp that Hazel had in her dining room?"

"The ugly one that looked like a sunken ship or something?"

"That's the one. That was also in the box. Hazel hated absolutely everything, but Otto insisted that they had to use it all so as not to offend his mother. He wanted to use the wallpaper in the sitting room, but she managed to persuade him that it would be better in the bedroom that his parents would use when they visited. She also managed to get one of the children to break the lamp eventually."

"I don't recall Otto's family ever visiting."

"As far as I know, they never did. They did plan to visit several times, but they always ended up cancelling for some reason or another. Hazel told me that after the third or fourth time she simply stopped worrying about them coming and assumed they were going to cancel."

A knock on the door interrupted the conversation.

"Oh, goodness, that's my friend," Bessie said. "We need to go if we're going to get to Ramsey in time for our booking."

"Ring me tomorrow," Esther said. "I'm going to ring everyone I know and find out what's happening with Hazel. It must be something quite dreadful, because she would never have agreed to sell the house otherwise."

"Do you have a number for Delores?"

"I don't. I don't have one for Laura, either."

"Neither do I, but perhaps we need to reach out to one of them."

"I do have a number for Patrick, but the last time we spoke, he thought I was the Queen. He was terribly confused, the poor dear."

"Yes, I'd heard he wasn't well."

Someone knocked again.

"My goodness, you go," Esther said quickly. "Ring me tomorrow, or I'll ring you."

Bessie put the phone down and rushed to the door. Andrew grinned at her.

"Ready for dinner?"

Bessie nodded. "I was talking to Esther." She slid on her shoes and then grabbed her handbag. After locking her door, she followed Andrew to his hire car. Matt was behind the wheel of his car, waiting for them. Bessie climbed into the passenger seat of Andrew's car and waited until he was slowly driving away before she continued.

"After she heard my message, she rang Hazel. She got the same recorded message that I did about the number not being in service. She's going to ring a few friends and see if she can find out anything."

"Did she tell you when she'd last spoken to Hazel?"

"I didn't think to ask. We were trying to talk quickly because I knew I had to leave."

"I assume she's going to ring you if she learns anything."

"Yes. We've agreed to talk again tomorrow, whether she learns anything or not."

"Maybe we'll find out more when we tour the house."

Bessie sighed. "I can't help but hope that it's all a big misunderstanding."

They drove to Ramsey with Matt following behind. He parked next to Andrew in the Seaview's large car park and then quickly walked over to help Bessie out of the car.

"This is not what I was expecting," Matt said as they walked towards the building.

"What were you expecting?" Bessie asked.

Matt flushed. "I know you said it was the island's nicest hotel, but I wasn't expecting it to be this – I don't know – grand may be the right word."

"Wait until you see the inside," Andrew told him.

As they walked into the huge lobby, Matt gasped.

"Wow. This is spectacular," he said.

"Thank you," Jasper Coventry said from behind the reception desk.

Bessie smiled at the man who was both owner and

manager of the hotel. He and his partner, Stuart, had poured a fortune into the rundown hotel when they'd bought it, and Bessie knew Jasper never got tired of hearing people complimenting their efforts.

"Jasper, lovely to see you," Andrew said as Jasper walked out from behind the desk.

Jasper shook hands with Andrew and was introduced to Matt before he gave Bessie a hug.

"We've put you in the largest of the private dining rooms, and Chef has created a special menu for you," he told them as he released Bessie. "It has some of Bessie's favourite items and a few new things that Chef is considering adding to the regular menu. He thought your group would be the perfect one to try out his most creative ideas on."

"Lovely," Bessie said. "Although I may choose one of my favourites rather than anything new."

Jasper nodded. "Of course, of course. I'd love to show you to the dining room myself, but I'm on my own at the desk right now. I'm desperately trying to hire more staff, but it isn't easy finding just the right people. I'm afraid I'm finding it difficult to trust anyone these days."

Bessie frowned. "What a shame."

"Last month we discovered that one of the staff was selling guests' credit card numbers," Andrew told Matt as they walked along the long corridor that led to the restaurant. "Jasper thinks of everyone he employs as family, so he was very upset to learn that someone he'd trusted was doing something illegal."

Matt nodded. "It must be similar to finding out that your wife married you only for her own personal gain and never really loved you," he said bitterly.

Andrew opened his mouth to reply, but Matt held up a hand. "Sorry, it's okay. I'll shut up now."

Before Andrew could reply, they'd reached the door to the restaurant.

"Ah, Inspector Cheatham, we have your party in the Sunset Room," Peter Christian, the restaurant's assistant manager, said.

"Sunset Room?" Bessie repeated.

Peter shrugged. "Jasper thought it might be useful to name the private dining rooms. Last week he was calling them by colour names, but this week he's changed them to Sunset, Sunrise, and Blue, which is left over from last week."

Bessie laughed. "I'll have to speak to him about it. He should give the rooms Manx names if he wants to name them."

"That's a good idea. I'll mention it to him if I see him before you do," Peter said. "Obviously, I'll tell him it was your idea."

He escorted them to a large private dining room with huge windows that showcased the beach outside.

"The view is different in the summer months," Peter said, somewhat apologetically, as he nodded towards the beach.

Bessie stared at the cluster of people who were lying on the sand almost right outside the window. A small boy rushed towards them, waving his arms and laughing. Bessie took a step backwards as he reached the glass and then began rubbing wet sand all over it.

"I am sorry," Peter said.

Bessie laughed. "As he isn't your child, you've nothing for which to apologise. We'll be too busy enjoying dinner to worry about what's happening on the beach, anyway."

Peter didn't look happy, but he didn't argue. Instead, he gave them all their specially prepared menus and rushed away to get them drinks. Bessie read through the menu and then looked at Andrew.

"I want six different things on this menu," she said.

He nodded. "I was thinking something similar. Let's at least get two different things and share."

"Can we do that three ways?" Matt asked. "I'll happily eat any three things on this menu."

Andrew laughed. "Maybe we should just order one of everything and everyone can try a bit of each dish."

In the end, they ordered two of everything on the menu and turned dinner into something of a buffet. Bessie thoroughly enjoyed her evening with her dear friends and their families. Matt seemed happy enough meeting everyone. By the time they left the Seaview, all feeling very full after having also ordered two of every pudding, Bessie had almost forgotten about how worried she was about her friend Hazel.

CHAPTER 4

"I'm already having second thoughts," Andrew said as he drove himself and Bessie towards Douglas the next morning.

"Oh? We haven't even seen any of the houses yet," Bessie replied.

"It's the drive. I'm not certain I'd be happy in Douglas."

"You could easily find a hotel in Douglas to host our monthly meetings, and Harry and Charles probably wouldn't mind staying in Douglas. There are several large hotels on the promenade that could accommodate them and our meetings."

"But that would mean you and Doona and John and Hugh would have to come into Douglas for the meetings. Ramsey is much more convenient for you."

"Douglas is still a good deal more convenient for us than it is for you or for Harry and Charles. You all have to travel to the island every month," Bessie pointed out.

Andrew shrugged. "We'll see." He glanced over at Bessie. "I think I'd much prefer to find something closer to you, though."

Bessie felt her cheeks flood with colour. Unable to think of an appropriate response, she turned her head and looked out the window at the passing scenery. "Nearly every inch of this island is beautiful," she said a short while later.

"You aren't wrong. That's one of the reasons why I'm considering buying a property here. Eventually I'm going to retire properly and, when I do, I may decide to move out of London. There's a part of me that would love to live here."

"You'd miss your family."

"Ah, but I've been working on that. Helen is already falling in love with the island, and now it's Matt's turn to experience everything it has to offer. If I can get one or two of my children to move here, the rest of the family would have to come and visit regularly."

Bessie chuckled. "I didn't realise having your children come with you was all part of a master plan."

"I wish I could tell you that I don't really need them here, but my health concerns are, unfortunately, all too real. But that doesn't mean I'm not trying to take advantage of their presence to try to sell them on the island."

"If I can do anything to help, let me know."

"Perhaps tomorrow morning we can take Matt around one of the castles or some other historical site. I want him to see as much of the island as possible."

"Is this the right address?" Bessie asked as Andrew pulled to a stop in front of a small cottage.

He shut off the car and then reached into the back to pick up the paperwork he'd left there. "It's the address on the paperwork."

"The cottage looked a good deal nicer in the pictures than it does in person."

Andrew nodded. "It's very cute."

"Indeed, but is it somewhere you'd want to live?"

They got out of the car and slowly approached the front

of the building. As they walked, the front door swung open, and a pretty brunette smiled out at them. She looked no more than thirty, in large glasses with bright red frames. Her hair was pulled into a high ponytail, and she was wearing dark grey trousers with a blouse that matched her glasses.

"Mr. Cheatham? Hello. I'm Betty Jones. Jacob had a last-minute meeting, so he asked me to take his place today. It's lovely to meet you. Jacob has told me all about you and your search for the perfect property on the island."

Andrew nodded. "It's lovely to meet you. This is my friend, Bessie Cubbon."

"Oh, everyone on the island knows Aunt Bessie," the woman replied. "My cousins grew up in Laxey, and they used to talk about her all the time." She smiled at Bessie. "Apparently your cottage is a magical place full of wondrous things to eat and drink. My cousin Lois insisted that it smelled of roses all year long and that if you remembered to say 'please' and 'thank you,' you always got an extra biscuit."

Bessie laughed. "Lois Jones?" she asked.

"No, she's Lois Henderson, or rather, she was when she was younger. She's Lois Daniels now, and she lives in Birmingham," Betty told her.

"Lois Henderson?" Bessie echoed. "Was she blonde and did she have two older brothers? If I'm remembering correctly, neither of them ever remembered to say please or thank you."

Betty laughed loudly. "That sounds exactly right. One of them is an advocate now and the other one moved to America and joined the circus."

"My goodness, shall I guess which is which?" Bessie thought for a moment. "Lawrence was always the more serious of the two, whereas Leonard had more of a wild side. Having said that, I always felt as if Lawrence wanted to be more like Leonard. I can see either of them doing either thing, really, but it would make me happy to hear that Lawrence is the one who joined the circus."

Betty laughed again. "Lawrence is the one who joined the circus. He started out as a clown, but he's now their business manager, which shouldn't surprise you. He's still a clown, too, though, at least once in a while."

"And Lois is in Birmingham? I didn't know that," Bessie said.

"Oh, aye, she went to uni over there and then decided to stay. Her mum and dad ended up moving across to be closer to her and Leonard, although they spend a few months every summer following Lawrence's circus."

"What fun that must be."

Betty nodded and then looked at Andrew. "Aunt Bessie is everyone's favourite auntie – well, everyone who grew up in Laxey, anyway. I grew up in Foxdale and missed out on spending hours and hours in Bessie's kitchen, telling her all of my problems. The way Lois tells it, she spent more of her teen years in your cottage than anywhere else."

Bessie shook her head. "I don't remember Lois staying with me for more than an odd night or two. Quite a lot of Laxey teens did the same. There weren't all that many that stayed with me more regularly."

"I don't suppose you have time for sobbing teenagers any longer," Betty replied. "Not with all the work you're doing solving cold cases. I couldn't believe it when I read the article in the local paper. Imagine having a retired old lady on a cold case unit, I thought."

"It's been rather brilliant," Andrew said before Bessie could reply. "We've had a great deal of success, and Bessie has been a large part of that success."

"I don't suppose you can tell me anything about any of your cases," Betty said. "I love watching true crime shows on the telly."

"I'm sorry, but everything we do is classified," Andrew told her.

"Oh, well, should we look at a few houses, then?" Betty asked.

Andrew looked at Bessie, who was still frowning at having been called old. "Ready?" he asked.

Bessie nodded. "The photos made this house look nicer than it is," she said.

Betty shrugged. "We have a photographer who takes all of our photos. He's very good at getting just the right angles to make properties look their very best."

"I would suggest that the photo in the listing dates from some years ago," Bessie replied.

"Ah, well, sometimes the owners have old photos of their homes that they particularly want us to include in the listing," Betty said. "We do everything we can to accommodate them, of course."

"Of course," Andrew murmured.

"But come inside and see how adorable this cottage is," Betty suggested. She stepped back and then stopped. "Actually, I'll let you explore on your own," she said, walking out of the cottage.

Andrew let Bessie go first. She walked into the small sitting room and looked around.

"It's tiny," she whispered, keeping an eye on Betty, who was standing in the doorway.

"It's not much smaller than the holiday cottage," Andrew replied.

Bessie nodded and then walked further into the room. "It's neat and tidy, but it could do with a coat of paint and new carpets." She kept walking, through the door at the back of the room.

The kitchen was also quite small, and the large table in the corner only made it feel even tinier. Bessie frowned.

"You'd probably want to replace all of the appliances. I believe they're older than mine. I doubt any of them still work," she said.

Andrew shrugged. "The price is low enough that I could have some work done in here."

"New countertops, new flooring, paint, new appliances," Betty said from the doorway. "All of that would go a long way to making this a beautiful and modern kitchen. It's perfectly functional the way it is, though."

"And I don't plan to actually do much cooking," Andrew added. "I probably would never bother doing anything in here."

Bessie walked into the next room. It was a small bedroom. Beyond that was another small bedroom before she reached a larger one.

"This is larger than the bedrooms in the holiday cottage," Andrew said when he joined her. "The other two are smaller, though. If I do buy a house here, I would hope that I would have visitors quite regularly. I'm not certain any of them would want to stay with me in either of those tiny bedrooms."

"The current owners have taken excellent care of the property," Betty said as she stuck her head into the room.

Bessie nodded. "It's clearly been well looked after, but it could do with some modernising."

"At least the bathroom fixtures are all white," Betty replied. "Some of these older properties have fixtures in all sorts of odd colours."

Bessie peeked into the small bathroom and then slowly made her way back to the sitting room at the front of the house.

"So, what do you think? The more you tell me what you liked and disliked, the better I'll be able to help you find your dream home," Betty said as she and Andrew followed Bessie into the room.

"It's too small," Andrew said. "It feels even smaller than the holiday cottage where I'm currently staying. The holiday cottage has a better layout, too, with many more windows. It's a lovely little cottage, and I'm certain someone would love to make it his or her home, but that someone isn't me, I'm afraid."

"We've a lot more to see," Betty replied. "I believe the flat is next. It may not be any larger than this, but it does have sea views. To my mind, that makes up for a lot."

"We'll see," Andrew replied.

"It was a lovely little cottage," Andrew said as they drove behind Betty towards the promenade.

"Little being the operative word."

"Exactly. I can't imagine my children or grandchildren being happy staying in those guest bedrooms."

"I think the layout was part of the problem. If I bought it, I think I'd remove all of the interior walls and start over again. I'd probably try to fit in only two bedrooms, but I'd make them both en-suite."

Andrew nodded. "There were odd bits of wasted space, and the bathroom was larger than it needed to be. It could be really special if someone put time and effort into it."

"And money."

"Yes, of course, and money."

Betty parked along the promenade in a large space right in front of the building with the flat for sale. Unfortunately, that was the only space anywhere near the building. Andrew drove up and down twice before he found a spot some distance away.

"You would think Betty would have wanted you to have that space," Bessie said as they walked back to find the woman.

"Should I tell her that the parking situation has put me off even looking at the flat?"

Bessie chuckled. "What a tempting thought. But you do want to see the flat, don't you?"

"I suppose so. As I said earlier, I'm not really sold on Douglas, though."

"There you are," Betty said loudly as they approached her. She was leaning against her car, tapping on her phone. When they reached her, she dropped the device into her pocket and smiled brightly at them.

"Now don't you worry about parking," she said. "This flat comes with its own space in the parking garage under the building."

"Just one space?"

Betty nodded. "Do you have more than one car?"

"No, but I am expecting to have guests quite regularly," Andrew replied.

"There's always parking along the promenade," Betty replied with a wave of her hand.

Bessie looked up and down and then frowned. "Except there isn't any at the moment."

Betty glanced around and then shrugged. "No doubt several spaces will all open up at once. By the time we come out, there probably won't be another car around anywhere."

Betty led them across the street and into the building.

"This used to be a luxury hotel," she told Andrew. "The owners had it converted into flats about five years ago."

Bessie looked around the small foyer. "I remember the hotel."

Betty smiled nervously. "Perhaps luxury is a slight exaggeration."

Bessie looked at Andrew, who chuckled. "Let's see the flat, then," he suggested.

They walked through the foyer into a short corridor. Betty stopped and pushed the button to call the lift.

"It seems likely that several other hotels along the promenade will be getting converted into flats over the next few years," she said. "The island doesn't get as many tourists as it did formerly. Even when the island was at its peak as a tourist destination, the winter months were always quieter."

"Having fewer hotels will make things difficult during the racing," Bessie suggested.

"A lot of people are renting out their homes now," Betty replied. "We can help with that if it's something you'd like to consider," she told Andrew. "You'd be shocked to hear what people are willing to pay for a nice property in a good location for TT Fortnight."

"I don't think I'd be interested in letting people stay in my house," Andrew replied.

The lift doors opened with a soft "ping." The trio went inside.

"The flat is on the third floor," Betty said as she pushed the button. "It's on the front of the building, so you do get sea views."

The lift opened into a long corridor. Bessie frowned as she walked out of the car.

"These carpets must be older than five years," she said.

"While the flats were modernised at great expense, some parts of the building were given less attention," Betty admitted.

"So these are the same carpets that were here when this was a hotel?" Bessie asked.

"I don't know that for certain, but that may be the case," Betty replied.

They stopped in front of a door and Betty unlocked it.

"You go in and have a look around," she suggested. "I'll wait here."

"That's what she said last time," Andrew murmured as he and Bessie walked into a small sitting room.

"This is nice, but the windows are awfully small," Bessie said. She walked over and looked outside. "You can see the sea, but it feels quite far away, really."

Andrew joined her. "It certainly seems far away compared to the cottage in Laxey that's right on the beach. The promenade is quite wide and puts a lot of distance between us and the water."

"The kitchen is really just a wall of appliances," Bessie said as she walked to the left.

"It's all that I need, though. I won't be doing much cooking."

Bessie opened a few cupboards and then turned back around. "It's hard to visualise how you'd use the space. I'm certain it feels larger than it is because it's empty."

Andrew nodded. "I'd want a table and chairs somewhere and then a couch and some chairs, maybe a coffee table or some side tables. I'm afraid that I wouldn't be able to see the water if I was sitting down in here, though."

Bessie walked to the opposite wall and opened the door in it. The short corridor had four doors opening off of it, two on either side. She looked at two small bedrooms on one side and then a larger bedroom and a small bathroom on the other.

"It's a shame the largest bedroom doesn't have any windows," she said as she and Andrew walked back into the sitting room. "It should have been on the opposite side of the corridor."

"But then you'd have the bathroom on that side, too, and you wouldn't want windows in the bathroom," Andrew replied. "And the two smaller bedrooms would feel a lot smaller if they didn't have any windows."

"What do you think?" Betty asked as they walked out of the flat.

"It's nice, but it's not exactly what I want," Andrew told her.

"Why? The more I know, the more I can help," she replied.

Andrew spent the ride back down in the lift running through a few of the issues that he had with the flat.

"I think the next house is going to be perfect for you," Betty said when they reached her car. "I'll meet you there."

Bessie and Andrew made the long walk back to Andrew's car.

"You asked me to remind you that you can't afford the next house," Bessie said as Andrew started the car.

"But now that I'm seeing what I can afford, I'm rethinking my budget. If I have to stretch it a bit in order to get what I want, well, maybe I'll have to consider it."

The house wasn't far away. Andrew parked on the street outside and they sat in the car and studied the house for a moment.

"It's cute, and it's obviously been very well looked after," Andrew said after a moment.

"It's almost too perfect," Bessie said. "Someone put a lot of time and effort into every little detail."

They walked to the door and Andrew knocked.

"Ah, sorry, I was just switching on lights and things," Betty said when she opened the door. "Come in, come in."

They walked into a tiny entryway.

"There's a storage cupboard here for coats and whatnot," Betty told them, opening the door. "And there's a cloakroom. The sitting room is on the left."

They strolled through the comfortable sitting room and the small dining room. The kitchen was even more beautiful in person than it had been in pictures. The first floor had two small bedrooms and a larger one, along with a spacious family bathroom.

"It's lovely," Andrew said as they exited the house. "It's just a bit outside my budget."

"Prices are always negotiable," Betty replied. "We can put in an offer and see what they say."

"First, let's take a look at the last house on the list," Andrew suggested.

Betty nodded. "I'll see you there," she said.

Andrew and Bessie got into the car. Andrew was quick to start the engine and pull away. After a moment, he glanced at Bessie.

"That house was almost creepily perfect."

"I kept wanting to move something, anything, out of place," Bessie admitted. "I felt as if I'd wandered into a movie set or something."

"Of course, it would feel quite different if I bought it. I don't have nearly as many unnecessary cushions, for a start."

Bessie laughed. "There were cushions everywhere, and they were all plump and perfectly positioned."

"I assume you don't know the owners of that house."

"I don't believe I do. I kept looking at the pictures that were scattered around the place, but I didn't recognise anyone in any of them."

"Really? I recognised the woman in the picture on the bedside table in the green bedroom."

"You did?"

Andrew nodded. "She's a model and actress from London. We met once, years ago now. I do believe one of her jobs was to pose for the sample pictures that manufacturers put in photo frames when they put them up for sale."

"So the pictures around the house weren't of the owners," Bessie said. "They were just the pictures that came with the frames."

"I believe so."

"No wonder I didn't recognise anyone," Bessie laughed.

Her laughter stopped abruptly as Andrew turned a corner and Hazel's house came into view.

"I do hope everything is okay," she said softly as Andrew parked on the street a short distance from Hazel's door.

CHAPTER 5

Andrew knocked. When the door swung open, Bessie gasped.

"Ah, good morning," the man in the doorway said. "Here to look at the house, are you?"

"Alan Collins? What are you doing here?" Bessie demanded.

He frowned at her. "Have we met?"

"Yes, of course we've met," Bessie replied. "The last time I saw you, you were running away from a house that you should not have been showing, shouting 'Fire!'"

Alan frowned. "I believe you've confused me with someone else. Perhaps your memory isn't as sharp as it used to be."

"I was there, too," Andrew interjected. "And I remember it exactly as Bessie does."

"Sorry," Betty said as she rushed towards them. "I got held up in traffic and then I had to park on the next street."

"Yes, the parking situation isn't ideal," Andrew said. "I was fortunate to find a space nearby, but it was the only space available."

"Yes, well, here we are, then," Betty said. "It's a lovely house in a charming older neighbourhood."

"And the parking isn't usually bad," Alan added. "I got a space right outside when I got here." He nodded towards the car that Bessie recognised as his. It was literally right in front of Hazel's door.

"Why is he here?" Bessie asked Betty.

Betty smiled. "Sometimes sellers prefer to have their agent present when potential buyers are looking at a property. Alan is here to answer any questions you might have about this wonderful Victorian terraced house."

"I was surprised to see the listing, as I know the owner," Bessie said as Alan took a step backwards and waved them inside.

"Of course you do," Alan muttered.

"How lovely," Betty said. "I'm certain she's quite sorry to be leaving such a lovely home."

"Is she?" Bessie asked Alan.

"Is who what?" Alan replied.

"Is the owner sad to be leaving her home?" Bessie asked.

"Oh, of course, yeah, of course. She's been here a long time, but she's, um, well, you know," he stammered.

Bessie stared hard at him. "No, I don't know. She's what?"

"You did say that you know her," Alan replied. "Perhaps you should ask her."

"Oh, I intend to," Bessie replied, watching Alan's face as the colour left it.

"This is obviously the sitting room," Betty said. "What do you think?" she asked Andrew.

"It's beautiful," he replied. "It feels spacious, in part thanks to the large windows."

"There's a dining room through here, and then the kitchen," Alan said, leading them from room to room.

"The kitchen could do with some modernising, but the

appliances are fairly new, and everything is in good condition," Betty said.

Bessie pulled open the refrigerator and frowned at the contents. Andrew looked over her shoulder.

"That's one of my favourite cheeses," he told Bessie, gesturing towards the wrapped block of cheese on one of the shelves.

She nodded. "Obviously, there's plenty of room for milk, cheese, butter, meats, everything you'd need to put in here." She pushed the door shut and then opened a cupboard at random.

"Lots of space for cereal boxes and other food packets," Andrew said.

"There's plenty of room for one person living on his own," Betty said.

Andrew nodded. "The bedrooms are upstairs, then?"

"There are two smaller ones on the first floor and then a larger one on the second floor," Alan told him. "You can go and have a look yourselves."

Bessie and Andrew climbed the stairs to the first floor. Both bedrooms were plainly furnished, the beds unmade. Bessie checked both wardrobes and found them empty. Things were different in the second-floor bedroom, though. A pink and purple duvet covered the bed. Two large cuddly toys rested against a large stack of pillows at the head of the bed. The large wardrobe was full of clothes.

"Hazel's?" Andrew asked in a whisper.

"I believe so, but I can't be certain, not without going through them more carefully."

"And we don't have time for that."

"It looks as if someone was just in here, getting ready for the day," Bessie said as she walked into the en-suite bathroom.

"It still smells faintly of soap or shampoo," Andrew said as he joined her. "Someone took a shower in here this morning." He opened the door to the shower and nodded. "The floor is still wet."

"What is going on?" Bessie asked.

"How are you doing?" Alan shouted from somewhere.

"We're just coming down now," Andrew replied.

He and Bessie walked back down the stairs silently. Alan and Betty were standing in the sitting room, waiting for them.

"What do you think?" Betty asked.

"It's lovely, and it could be just what I need," Andrew replied. "I may want to see it again in a day or two. My son is on the island with me, and I'd very much like to get his opinion on the property."

"Of course, of course," Betty said.

Alan cleared his throat. "We need as much notice as possible, please. We need to make all of the necessary arrangements with the owner."

"Yes, of course," Andrew replied.

Alan and Betty escorted them out of the house together.

"I'll keep sending you properties as they're listed," Betty said. "Ring me immediately if you see anything you like."

Bessie was silent as Andrew spoke to Betty for a few minutes. When he unlocked the car, she climbed inside without doing anything more than giving Alan and Betty a quick wave.

"That was interesting," Andrew said as they drove away.

"Hazel is still living there."

"Someone is still living there."

"It felt as if Hazel is still living there."

"The refrigerator and the cupboards were full. Someone went shopping quite recently."

Bessie nodded. "I need to ring Esther and see if she's managed to learn anything."

"Do you want to go back to Laxey to do that?"

"I don't need to go anywhere. I can ring her from my mobile."

Andrew pulled his car into one of Douglas's multi-storey car parks and found a space. "Ring Esther, and then we'll have a wander around the shops until time for lunch."

Bessie dug out her phone and dialled Esther's number. She frowned when she reached her answering machine.

"It's Bessie. Please ring me back," was all that she said in her message. She gave her friend her mobile number before ending the call. As she put her phone away, she frowned at Andrew. "I feel as if we should be doing more."

"What else can we do?"

"I don't know."

"Let's take a walk through town while we both try to think," he suggested. "If either of us comes up with an idea, we won't be very far from the car."

They walked up and down the high street twice, looking in shop windows and chatting about nothing. Although she tried, Bessie couldn't think of anyone else to ring about Hazel.

"Where does she usually shop?" Andrew asked as they turned around at the end of the street.

"I've no idea. There's a ShopFast not far from her house, but there are several other shops that aren't much farther away. That's the nice thing about living in Douglas, of course."

Andrew nodded. "Shall we have a look around the bookshop?"

Bessie hesitated and then sighed. "I never turn down the chance to look around a bookshop."

Half an hour later, they emerged, each carrying a bag of books.

"Let's put these in the car and then have some lunch," Andrew suggested.

They went to one of Bessie's favourite places. As they waited for their food to arrive, Andrew looked around the room.

"Are there any particular places that you know Hazel enjoys going?" he asked.

Bessie sighed. "I wish I did. I feel as if I know nothing about her, really. We've been friends for many decades, but I know very little about her day-to-day life now. I feel as if I'm letting her down badly."

"What about medical care? Who is her GP?"

"I know she used to see Dr. Quayle. He had his surgery one street over from her, but he retired in the late eighties. I remember Hazel complaining about the man who replaced him. I'm certain she found somewhere else to go, but I don't know that she ever said where. These are all things I'll ask Esther, though, when she rings me back."

Andrew patted her hand. "I know it's worrying, but we're doing everything we can to find her, short of reporting her missing."

Bessie quickly shook her head. "I don't want to report her missing. She may well have simply had her number changed. The last thing we need to do is bring the police into this."

"I am the police," Andrew said with a grin.

Bessie chuckled. "Yes, of course, but you know what I meant. Let's see what Esther has to say and then decide whether we need to worry more or not."

"That seems a good plan. We've a unit meeting in an hour, anyway."

Bessie nodded. "Is it murder again?" she asked.

Andrew shook his head. "Not this time. At least, I hope not."

"Another missing person? So far we've found one alive and well and the other, well, not alive. I really hope this case has another happy ending."

"That would be nice, although I do consider finding and putting killers behind bars the next best thing to a happy ending."

"Yes, of course."

They decided against pudding, as the Seaview always provided biscuits or something nicer for the unit meetings. As they drove north towards Ramsey, Bessie kept the conversation light. When they reached the hotel, Andrew parked and then took Bessie's hand.

"If Esther rings during the meeting, just let me know and we'll stop so you can talk to her," he said.

"I can't do that."

"Of course you can."

Bessie didn't bother to argue, but she had no intention of interrupting the cold case unit meeting to speak to her friend. After having never held a paying job in her life, the small stipend that she was receiving from the work she did with the unit made it feel far more important than anything else in her life.

"Ah, good afternoon," Sandra Cook said from behind the reception desk.

Bessie smiled at the young woman. "Good afternoon."

"Mr. Coventry has put you in the penthouse today," she told them. "And Chef has sent up some tarts for you to try. He and the pastry chef had a bit of a disagreement about tart fillings, so they've each made several different varieties, and now they need people to try them all and tell them which ones are best."

"Wonderful," Andrew said.

Sandra made a face. "It's not so wonderful for me, as I've

been trying to mediate between the two all day. Still, it's a nice treat for you."

Bessie and Andrew took the lift to the top floor. The penthouse meeting room was only a few steps away. Bessie smiled when she saw the table at the back of the room.

"Lemon, apple, custard, pear and almond, chocolate, and even mince pies," she said happily as she began filling a plate.

"Mince pies? What a wonderful treat for August," Andrew replied. He filled his own plate, mostly with the traditional Christmas sweet, and then set it on the table. After pouring himself a cup of coffee, he sat down and removed a large stack of envelopes from his briefcase.

Bessie sat down next to him with her plate of tarts and a cup of tea. "Now I want to have a peek," she said, nodding at the envelopes.

"But you'll wait for the others, because it's only fair."

Bessie laughed. "I don't know that anyone would actually complain if I were allowed to see the file early."

"Let's not find out," Andrew suggested, winking at Bessie.

She pulled out her mobile and stared at the screen. "I wish Esther would ring."

"Try her again."

"I don't want to be a bother. She may not be home, or she may be busy. I'll wait and try her again after the meeting if she hasn't rung me back by then."

"Sandra said there were tarts," Hugh said as he pushed the door open.

"There are, several different varieties," Bessie confirmed.

"I'm as excited as a little kid at Christmas," Hugh laughed. "And there are even mince pies. It is Christmas!"

He was still stacking tarts into piles on his plate when John and Doona arrived. Harry wasn't far behind.

"Have a few tarts," Bessie suggested as the man headed to a chair that would put his back to the wall.

"I'm good," he replied as he sat down.

Charles arrived a moment later. He poured himself a cup of coffee and then sat down next to Harry.

'Good afternoon," Andrew began once everyone was sitting around the table. "I hope you all enjoyed dinner last night."

"It was wonderful," Bessie said.

"Grace really enjoyed getting to know everyone better, and Aalish seemed to have had fun. She fell asleep in the car on the way home and didn't wake up until after eight. I told Grace that we need to keep her up late more often," Hugh said.

John and Andrew both shook their heads.

"If you have her in a good routine, don't change it too often," John said.

"That's exactly what Grace told me. She said it's going to be especially important to keep Aalish's routine as we get ready for the new baby."

"She's right. The new baby is going to change everything," Andrew told him.

"I still haven't forgotten how difficult the sleepless nights were. I'm sometimes surprised that we decided to do it again," Hugh said with a laugh.

"*I* still remember how difficult the sleepless nights were," Andrew told him.

Everyone laughed.

"So, what is it this time?" Charles asked. "Murder again?"

"No, actually, it's another missing person case," Andrew replied. "Or rather, missing persons."

"Oh? That complicates things," Charles said. "Parent and child or a couple?"

"Parent and child," Andrew told him. "A young woman of twenty-three, Michelle Keller. She and her two-year-old daughter, Dazaray, disappeared ten years ago."

"Spell the daughter's name, please," Harry asked.

Andrew spelled it twice. "Michelle and her daughter were living in Dover at the time of their disappearance. Inspector Sherry Walters recently relocated to Dover after several years working in Derby. She's been assigned to missing persons, and as it has been quiet, she's been going back through unsolved cases. She's taken a keen interest in Michelle and Dazaray."

"Two-year-olds are difficult to hide," Charles said. "They're noisy and inquisitive, and they tend to be very active as well."

"Who reported Michelle and Dazaray missing?" John asked.

"Her parents, Stanley and Jessica Keller. Michelle and Dazaray lived with them, but they often spent nights with Michelle's boyfriend, Luke Sharp. Apparently, Michelle was usually very good at letting them know when she was going to be staying with Luke, but she sometimes forgot to ring them. When she and Dazaray didn't come home one night in July 1991, her parents simply assumed that they were staying with Luke."

"But they weren't," John said.

Andrew shook his head. "When they didn't come home the next night, Jessica rang Luke. He claimed that Michelle and Dazaray had left to go home the previous evening around seven."

"Claimed?" Doona echoed. "Michelle's parents didn't believe him?"

"Actually, Michelle's parents did believe him. That's why they immediately rang the police and reported the pair missing. I won't go into too much detail now. You can read all of the statements for yourselves."

"Was Luke Dazaray's father?" John asked.

"No, he was not," Andrew replied. "Her father had been Michelle's first serious boyfriend. They were together from the time she was sixteen. Sadly, he passed away from a rare and aggressive cancer not long after she found out that she was pregnant."

"So she didn't run away with him," Doona said.

"There's no evidence that she ran away at all. There's also no evidence to suggest any other solution. It's a very frustrating case. Sherry told me that she's become rather obsessed with it. She can't help but feel as if someone missed something somewhere along the way."

"Obviously, Luke was questioned," Charles said.

"He was. You have a copy of his original statement and also the statement that was taken from him a year later. Everyone involved was questioned at the time and then questioned again the following July. Sherry is going to speak to them all a third time once we send her a list of questions we want asked."

"So we don't have recent updates on the suspects?" Bessie asked.

"Not yet. Sherry doesn't want to talk to everyone multiple times if she can help it," Andrew told her.

"Missing person cases are difficult," Charles said. "In some ways, they are harder for witnesses than murder investigations. The not knowing is a difficult thing to live with."

"So Luke was questioned. I assume the parents were also questioned," Harry said.

Andrew nodded. "Both parents were questioned. They gave the police the names of Michelle's two closest friends. April Page and Krista James were also questioned both when Michelle first disappeared and again a year later."

"Who else?" John asked.

"The police went door to door but didn't find anyone

who could help. Otherwise, there wasn't anyone else," Andrew said.

"Where did Michelle work?" Charles asked.

"She wasn't working. After she left school at eighteen, she worked for a short while at a local clothing shop, but then she and her boyfriend went travelling. His name was Dylan Smith, by the way. They went travelling, only returning to Dover when Dylan started feeling unwell. He passed away not long after they got back. According to her mother, Michelle had a difficult pregnancy and spent much of it on bed rest. Once Dazaray arrived, Michelle stayed at home to look after her. She'd been talking about finding a job once Dazaray turned two, but the little girl had had her birthday in June and Michelle still hadn't started actually looking for work."

"What can you tell us about Michelle's friends, then?" Charles asked.

"April was her closest friend. They'd known one another since childhood. According to April, she and Michelle didn't have any secrets from one another."

"So if Michelle did run away, April probably knows where she is," Charles said.

"We'll talk about the possibilities once you've all read the file," Andrew said.

"What about the other friend, Krista?" Doona asked.

"She and Michelle had worked together at the shop I mentioned earlier. Krista also had a son around the same age as Dazaray. Apparently, the two women used to take the children to the park and other local places together."

"Presumably, even if someone did know where Michelle had gone, no one admitted to it," Charles said. "Most people who choose to disappear have help, though. Either one of the witnesses lied to the police or Michelle had more friends than her family realised."

"Let's save that conversation for after you've all read the interviews," Andrew suggested. "For now, let's…" He stopped as Bessie's mobile began to ring.

"It's Esther," Bessie said, getting to her feet. "I'll take it outside."

CHAPTER 6

Bessie walked out into the corridor and then pushed the button to answer the call.

"Hello?"

"Bessie, hello. I'm sorry I missed you earlier. I had an appointment at Noble's. You know those always take far longer than they should. I was so annoyed when I finally got away that I took myself out for a nice lunch. I've only just walked in the door and listened to my answering machine."

"I hope there's nothing seriously wrong," Bessie said.

"Seriously wrong? Oh, because I was at Noble's? Oh, no, nothing seriously wrong. They just like to keep an eye on every little thing since my last surgery. Sometimes I think I spend more time at Noble's than I do at home, but it's quite nice there, really, for a hospital, I mean."

Bessie chuckled. "Yes, it's quite nice for a hospital, but I don't enjoy spending time there, either."

"But you rang to see if I'd heard anything further about Hazel, didn't you?"

"I did, yes."

"Sadly, I've not managed to find anyone who has spoken

THE KELLER FILE

to her lately. Several people mentioned speaking to her around Christmas or early in the new year, but I didn't find anyone who has spoken to her since the middle of January."

Bessie frowned. "That's worrying."

"I couldn't find anyone who had any contact information for either Laura or Delores, either. I did try ringing Patrick, but whoever answered the telephone wouldn't let me speak to him. She said that he was asleep and that I should ring back another time. I'll try him again after we're finished, actually."

"Do you know where she typically does her shopping?" Bessie asked.

"She used to go to ShopFast, but they stopped carrying something she particularly enjoyed, so she started going to the big shop on the quayside. Then she got mad at them for something else and started going to ShopFast again, but at a different location rather than the one near her house. The last time we spoke, she told me that she was shopping in town more."

Bessie named the large UK-based chain that had a shop in the centre of town.

"That's the one. She said their food was good, and if you bought the things that were about to expire, they weren't terribly expensive, either."

Bessie sighed. "They're probably too large and too busy to notice whether any particular customer has been in or not."

"Oh, I'd imagine they've no idea who shops there," Esther agreed.

"What about favourite restaurants?"

"I don't believe Hazel eats in restaurants very often. She's on a tight budget, but then, aren't we all? Restaurants are expensive. She did say something once about one of her granddaughters taking her to the place in Onchan that does all the different food on one plate. I believe it was for her birthday one year. I don't believe she goes anywhere regularly."

"Do you know who her GP is?"

"She used to see Dr. Quayle. Everyone in Douglas used to see Dr. Quayle. He was brilliant. I still miss him."

"So you don't know who she's been seeing since he retired?"

"She tried the man who took over the practice, Dr. Redmond or Redcoat or Redsomething. I tried him, too, but we both thought he was quite dreadful. He was always in a rush, and he never really seemed to care. I'd start telling him my symptoms and he'd shake his head and sigh and tell me that I was getting older or that most women had what he called female troubles. Then he'd write a prescription for something useless and move on to the next victim, er, patient."

"I believe he got struck off some years ago."

"He did. Hazel and I were both quite pleased about it, really."

"But you don't know where she's going now?"

"I seem to remember her complaining about Dr. Tennley, so I'm fairly certain she saw him for a while, but she may well have moved again since. As I said, she complained to me about him."

"Can you think of any other way we might find her?" Bessie asked. "Just because we can't find her doesn't mean she's actually missing, of course, but it's worrying, nevertheless."

"It is worrying. I'm going to go back through my address book and try ringing people who know people who know Hazel. I'll ring Patrick again, too. Maybe he'll know something, although I'm not certain I'll believe anything he says."

"Ring me back later tonight, please," Bessie said. "I'm

going to try ringing Dr. Tennley's surgery, although I doubt they will tell me anything."

"You need to have one of your police inspector friends ring. They'll talk to the police, even if they won't talk to you."

"You may be right about that," Bessie said.

"I'll ring you later," Esther promised.

Bessie dropped her phone into her pocket and walked back into the conference room.

"...up there and meet again tomorrow at the same time," Andrew was saying as Bessie slid into her seat.

"I'll see you all tomorrow, then," Harry said. He picked up the envelope that Andrew passed to him and then rushed out of the room.

Charles grabbed his envelope and quickly followed suit. Bessie watched as the others slowly gathered their things and headed for the door. Hugh filled a large takeaway box with tarts before he exited.

"You're a million miles away," Andrew said as the door shut behind Hugh. "What did Esther have to say?"

"Nothing useful," Bessie replied. She quickly repeated as much of the conversation as she could remember.

"I suppose the next step would be to ring the doctor's surgery," Andrew said.

"I can't imagine they'll tell me anything."

"Perhaps John can make an informal request for information," Andrew suggested. "We don't want to know anything about the woman's health. We'd simply like to know whether anyone there has seen or spoken to her lately."

"I hate to bother John with this."

"I can probably get the information for you, but it might take a bit longer. Would you like me to ring a friend and see what I can do?"

Bessie hesitated and then nodded. "It's all going to be

done very discreetly, isn't it? I don't want Hazel to think that I'm being nosy."

Andrew nodded and then pulled out his phone. While he was talking to his friend, Bessie walked back to the table and picked up a chocolate tart. She was enjoying it when the door opened and Jasper walked into the room.

"How were the tarts?" he asked when he reached her.

"They were all delicious," Bessie replied.

"But which was your favourite?"

"I can't pick just one. I loved the chocolate ones, and I loved the almond and pear ones."

Jasper laughed. "That's one from the pastry chef and one from the main chef. They aren't going to believe me when I tell them."

"Who isn't going to believe what?" Andrew asked as he joined them.

"Our chef and our pastry chef," Jasper explained. "Bessie picked two favourites and they each made one of them. Which was your favourite?"

"I need to pick two as well – the chocolate and the lemon," Andrew replied.

"And again, that's one from each of them. I should have you come down to the kitchen and tell them yourselves. They definitely won't believe me," Jasper said with a sigh.

They talked about the tarts all the way from the conference room, through the hotel, to the front door.

"We'll see you tomorrow," Andrew told Jasper.

"Perhaps your chefs could fight over cakes tomorrow," Bessie suggested. "Or American-style cookies."

Jasper laughed. "Don't be surprised if you get more tarts in increasingly odd flavours. Chef was muttering about caramel with sea salt and rosemary the last time I was in the kitchen."

Bessie thought about it for a moment. "That might actually be nice."

"You may find out tomorrow," Jasper said.

"You're very quiet," Andrew said to Bessie as he drove them back towards Laxey.

"I'm just thinking about Hazel, but I should be thinking about the case. What did I miss while I was talking to Esther?"

"Nothing much. Mostly, people asked questions, and I refused to answer them until after you've all read the case file."

Bessie laughed. "Isn't that how our first meetings always go?"

"Pretty much."

"Esther is supposed to ring me back later. While I wait, I'll start on the case file."

"What about dinner?"

"Do you and Matt want to have dinner at my cottage? I can put something together fairly quickly."

"I'm happy to do that, but I'm also happy to go out somewhere."

Bessie thought for a moment. "I think I'd rather make dinner at my cottage. I want to be there when Esther rings."

"Can I help in any way?"

"I'll make spaghetti," Bessie told him. "That takes only half an hour if I use sauce from a jar. If you want, come over around half five, you can help get everything ready for dinner at six."

Andrew pulled his car into the parking area outside of Bessie's cottage. "Matt isn't home yet. I'll ring him and see if he's planning to be back for dinner or not. Either way, I'll see you around half five."

Bessie let herself into her cottage, clutching the envelope with her copy of the file and thinking about Hazel. She put the kettle on and then looked up a number in the telephone directory.

"Wellness Surgery, this is Carla. How can I help you?" a voice said.

"Ah, Carla, this is Elizabeth Cubbon. How are you today?"

"Aunt Bessie? I'm fine. How are you?"

"Fine, fine," Bessie replied as she tried to place the voice. "Is this Carla Watson?"

"It is, aye. I've been working here for about three months now."

"I had no idea. Have you moved to Douglas, then?"

"Oh, aye, I have at that. Bobby got moved to the Douglas branch of the bank, and after him driving back and forth for a few months, we both agreed that we needed to move down here. I don't mind being a bit farther away from Mum, if I'm honest. But you didn't ring to talk about me. What can I do for you?"

"I'm trying to find a friend of mine, and I believe she might be a patient there. I do appreciate that you can't tell me anything about her health, but I was hoping you might be able to tell me whether she's been in to see anyone there lately or not. I'm a bit concerned about her, you see."

"Ah, I'm not allowed to give out any information at all about anything," Carla said. "But what's her name anyway?"

"Hazel Lace."

"Give me a minute and I'll see if anyone here knows her and is willing to say anything," Carla replied. "I'll just pop you on hold for a bit."

Bessie sipped her tea and listened to eighties pop music reimagined as jazz instrumentals while she waited. When her tea was gone, she opened her envelope and pulled out the case file. "It's smaller than normal," she muttered as she looked at the pile of papers in front of her.

"Ah, Bessie, I'm back," Carla said a moment later.

THE KELLER FILE

"Hello."

"Okay, so I talked to one of the nurses and she took a wee peek in the files. All I can tell you is that Ms. Lace is not a patient here."

"I'm quite certain she was a patient there once."

"I can neither confirm nor deny anything," Carla said. "But if she had been a patient here once, she hasn't been here in over a year."

"I don't suppose you could speculate on where she might have gone after she left your surgery?"

"I can't, although Seaside Medical Centre isn't far away. You might try ringing there."

"Thank you," Bessie said. "And good luck with your move to Douglas."

"Thanks. I think we're going to be very happy here."

Bessie put the phone down and then frowned. Carla had probably broken all sorts of rules. She'd feel terrible if Carla got into any trouble for what she'd done. Feeling reluctant to put anyone else in the same situation, she picked up her notebook and pen and turned her attention to the case file. She'd worry about Hazel again when Esther rang.

An hour later, she'd read through all of the interviews and taken a few pages of notes.

"There isn't anything there," she said, pushing her notebook away. "They simply disappeared."

Feeling frustrated and slightly headachy, she shut her eyes and slowly counted to ten. When that didn't seem to help, she kept counting. Her phone rang when she was at twenty-seven.

"Bessie? It's Esther. I spoke to Patrick."

"What did Patrick have to say?"

"Nothing useful in the slightest. I asked if he'd spoken to his mother lately and he seemed to think that I'd said that I was his mother. Then he started complaining about how he wasn't being given chocolate cake every day, and that I'd promised him that if he was a good boy, he'd get chocolate cake every day."

"Oh dear."

"In the end, I promised him that I'd speak to someone about cake and rang off."

Bessie sighed. "So that's another dead end."

"Indeed."

Bessie told her about the conversation she'd had with Carla. "I suppose I should ring Seaside next and see if I can learn anything there."

"Oh, don't do that," Esther said. "I know someone at Seaside. I'll ring her and then ring you back."

Esther ended the call before Bessie could reply. Sighing, she got up and got herself some headache tablets. It was nearly time for Andrew to arrive to start dinner, but she wasn't especially hungry.

"I'm frustrated," she told the man when he knocked on her door a short while later. "I've been through the entire case file, and it all feels a bit hopeless. There's barely anything in the file, for a start."

Andrew nodded. "Murder cases generate a lot more paperwork. In this case, we aren't even certain there was foul play involved."

"What else could it have been, though? Everything I read made it seem as if Michelle was simply a perfectly ordinary young woman with a small child. There wasn't anything in the file to suggest why she would have wanted to disappear."

Andrew nodded. "Which is why Sherry wants us to look at the case. She's convinced that the original investigation missed something."

Bessie opened her mouth to reply but was interrupted by the telephone.

"Hazel is now registered at Seaside," Esther told her. "But she hasn't been there to see anyone since late January."

"What about medications? I don't suppose you were able to find out if she's taking any medications that might need refilling."

"She isn't taking anything. I was shocked, because I'm taking a dozen different tablets every day, but apparently Hazel is fit and healthy."

"And missing."

"When my friend at the surgery heard that we were trying to find Hazel, she tried ringing her, but she got the same message we both got. Apparently, Patrick is listed as the person to contact in an emergency, which is no good to anyone."

Bessie sighed. "So what do we do now?"

"I was thinking of parking outside her house and watching it for a few hours, just to see who is going in and out, but then I remembered that I need the loo every thirty minutes these days," Esther said with a laugh.

"Thank you for everything you've done," Bessie said. "I'll talk to my friends with the police and see if they have any ideas."

"I wish I knew how to reach Delores or Laura."

"Maybe one of them will be easier to find."

"Laura is across, but Delores is on the island. I don't know where she's working these days, though."

"When I spoke to Hazel at Christmas, she told me that Delores was between jobs. She said something about her living with her boyfriend and not rushing to find something else."

"Now that you mention it, she said something similar to me. I got the impression that Hazel wasn't fond of Delores's boyfriend, but Delores has always made terrible choices when it comes to men."

"I can't remember Hazel mentioning the man's name."

"I don't recall it, either. Maybe that was why I thought she didn't care for him. Maybe she seemed to be avoiding saying it."

Bessie sighed. "I'll let you know if I find out anything."

"Likewise. I may ring a few people who I think know Patrick or Laura or Delores. Detective work is considerably more interesting than sitting around waiting until time for my next set of tablets, anyway. I've driven past the house a few times, and once I even went to the door, but no one answered. I'll keep trying that as well."

Bessie put the phone down and sighed again.

"No joy?"

She told Andrew everything that Esther had told her.

"It sounds as if Esther is enjoying the search, at least. Do you want me to ring a few people?"

"I don't want to start an official investigation or anything. I just want to know that Hazel is okay."

Andrew nodded. "I can ring a colleague in Leeds and see if he can track down Laura. It can all be done unofficially, at least for the time being."

"I'd appreciate that."

"You should ask John to see if he can find Delores," Andrew added.

Bessie made a face. "I was thinking that I might go and visit Patrick. Maybe he'd be less confused by an in-person visit."

"He might."

"And I might be able to find out from the staff at the care home how often his mother visits," Bessie added.

Andrew grinned at her. "That's a very good point. When did you want to go and see him?"

"Tomorrow afternoon, maybe, after the unit meeting? We were talking about going to see one of the castles in the morning, and I suspect Patrick probably sleeps late, anyway."

"Matt isn't back yet from wherever he's gone today, so I don't know if he's going to want to go visit a castle tomorrow or not, but if he doesn't, I'm certain we can find something to do to fill the morning."

Bessie nodded. "I suppose I'm hoping that Esther will ring back with some sort of news before we go to see Patrick. I'm not looking forward to visiting him, not if he's unlikely to remember me."

"It's very difficult, seeing people who were formerly friends struggle with memory issues."

"Let's talk about something else. Although I don't know what."

"We could talk about the case," Andrew suggested.

"Or we could talk about dinner," Bessie said as her stomach rumbled.

Andrew laughed. "Let's not just talk about it. Let's cook something."

Bessie started frying some minced beef in a pan while Andrew put water on to boil. She was just measuring the pasta when someone knocked on her door.

"Ah, good evening," Matt said when Bessie opened it. "Your island is amazingly beautiful."

"Thank you. Would you care to join us for dinner? We're making spaghetti," Bessie replied.

"I'd love that. I spent the day driving all over the island, and I have lots of questions for you."

"I hope I can answer them," Bessie laughed.

She added another serving of pasta to what she'd already measured and then put it all into the boiling water. Fifteen minutes later, she and the two men sat down to dinner.

"So I drove past a big castle in Castletown, which makes sense, I suppose. And then I drove past what looked like a castle or fortifications or something down in Peel. I tried to read the signs, but on unfamiliar roads, I didn't dare."

As they ate, Bessie told Matt all about Peel Castle and Castle Rushen.

"We thought you might like to visit one of them tomorrow morning," she added at the end.

"I'd love that. If it's up to me, we'll go to Castle Rushen. I think I'd much prefer a castle with walls and a roof."

"I hope you'll get to see both of them during your visit, but we can go to Castle Rushen tomorrow," Bessie agreed.

"And then we'll get lunch in Castletown before Bessie and I have to go to the Seaview for another meeting," Andrew added.

Bessie hadn't made a pudding, but she had ice cream in her freezer.

"This is perfect on a hot summer day," Matt said as he dug into his generous serving.

Andrew insisted on doing the washing-up, so Bessie and Matt chatted about some of the island's other historical sites while he worked. When he was done, he looked at Bessie.

"Fancy a walk on the beach?" he asked.

"Yes, please," Bessie replied.

CHAPTER 7

Matt laughed. "I'll walk with you as far as our cottage, but that's where I'm going to stop. After driving all over the island this morning, I parked in Douglas and walked up and down the promenade for hours this afternoon. I'm exhausted."

Bessie slid on her shoes and then followed Matt and Andrew out of the cottage.

"I'll see you in the morning," Matt said as he turned and walked back to the cottage he was sharing with his father.

Bessie and Andrew walked down to the water's edge and began a slow stroll past the holiday cottages. A few small children were chasing each other through the sand, and a group of teens were listening to music on a portable player right behind another cottage.

"It's busy out here tonight," Andrew remarked.

"Actually, for August, this isn't bad," Bessie told him. "I wonder if Maggie and Thomas are getting fewer bookings. I can remember summer days when I couldn't even venture outside because there were so many people out here."

Maggie and Thomas Shimmin had built the row of

holiday cottages years earlier, after Thomas had retired early from his career in banking. While they'd been very successful in their first few years of business, it seemed clear to Bessie that the cottages were less popular now than they had been just a year or two earlier.

"I don't believe any of the cottages are empty right now, although I suppose I could be mistaken."

"It doesn't look as if anyone is staying in that one," Bessie said, nodding towards the cottage that was second to last. "The curtains are all drawn and there aren't any lights on inside."

"You may be right."

"I'd hate to see the cottages become less successful. As much as I dislike it when the beach is crowded, the cottages are their livelihood for Maggie and Thomas. I'd hate to see Pat out of a job as well."

Andrew nodded. "I haven't seen Pat this visit yet."

"He's not actually on the island at the moment. He's gone across for his sister's wedding. He's due back later in the week, though."

"Bessie?" The voice seemed to come from above them.

Bessie stopped and looked up at the steps that led to Thie yn Traie, the huge mansion that was perched on the cliff above the beach. Elizabeth Quayle was slowly making her way down the stairs towards them.

"Hello," Bessie said when the young woman finally reached the bottom of the last of the series of interconnected stairways.

"Hi," Elizabeth replied softly.

"What's wrong?" Bessie asked.

The other woman shrugged. "Nothing, really. I'm just – well, I suppose I just don't know what I am."

Bessie frowned. "What's happened?"

Elizabeth glanced at Andrew. "I suppose you know all about everything that's gone wrong in my life," she said.

He glanced at Bessie and then looked back at Elizabeth. "I know that you used to have a very successful party planning business on the island and that you often worked with Andy Caine, who's a brilliant young chef."

Elizabeth nodded. "I should have known better than to mix business and pleasure, really. If I hadn't fallen madly in love with Andy, things would be so much better. But I had to go on holiday with my parents. After everything that happened after the murder, they needed to get away and my mother needed me. I'll never regret going, because then Mum fell ill and really needed me. I just wasn't expecting Andy to get engaged to someone else while I was gone."

"None of us were expecting that," Bessie said. "But none of us knew anything about Jennifer Johnson before you left the island."

"And even if we had, none of us could have expected her to be a con artist who would fabricate evidence that I'd cheated on Andy and had a secret baby," Elizabeth said. "Even now, I still can't quite believe that it happened. It's like something out of a movie or something."

"As photos become increasingly easy to manipulate, I expect such things to become more common," Andrew said. "The days of using photographs as evidence for anything seem to be disappearing fast."

"Too bad Andy didn't realise that a few months ago," Elizabeth said.

"The last time we spoke, you were thinking about going with him to look at a house," Bessie said. "I offered to go with you."

Elizabeth sighed. "I was all set to agree, and to drag you along, but then Mum took a bit of a turn, and we ended up going across so she could see an expert. We've only been back on the island for a few days."

"I didn't realise that. I hope your mother is feeling better now."

"She is, and she's sorry she still isn't up to seeing you. You're her closest friend on the island. Actually, you're her closest friend anywhere, but right now the only people she's seeing are her nurses and her family. We aren't even letting Jonathan see her, to try to protect her from germs."

Jonathan Hooper was the family's butler. Bessie had known him as a child, and she knew he was devoted to the family who now employed him.

"My goodness, I'm so sorry."

"We're probably overreacting, but she gave us quite a scare. As I said, she's better now, but she has a long way to go before she'll be back to normal."

"And that means you've had to put your life on hold again."

"It hasn't been that bad. I'd agreed to plan a handful of weddings, but the earliest is in the autumn. I managed to stay in touch with all of my brides and venues and whatnot while we were away, mostly thanks to email and lots of time on the telephone. The only thing I couldn't do was look at that house with Andy."

"Do you know if he's made an offer or not?"

"He hasn't done anything. He and Jonathan are talking nearly every day now because he keeps ringing to talk to me, but I don't want to talk to him."

"Do you want to go and see the house? I can't go tomorrow, but I could go the next day."

Elizabeth shrugged. "Part of me really wants to go, and part of me wants to stay as far away from Andy Caine as I can possibly get. While being away with Mum was difficult, in some ways it was a relief because wherever I went, I never had to worry that I'd bump into Andy. This island can feel very small when you're trying to avoid someone."

Bessie nodded. "I know exactly what you mean."

"Really?" Elizabeth looked at her curiously.

"Why don't you think about it? I'll leave the morning free, not tomorrow, but the day after. Ring me if you want to go and look at the house."

"What do you think I should do?"

"You have to do what feels right to you, but you know you won't be able to avoid Andy forever."

Elizabeth sighed. "I could just move to Idaho or something."

"Idaho?"

She laughed. "It was the first thing that popped into my mind. I don't even know where Idaho is, though."

"It's been a while since I studied US geography. It's somewhere in the middle of the country, I believe."

"I can't go and live in Idaho, though. Mum still needs me, and she doesn't want to be anywhere other than here."

Bessie pulled the woman into a hug. "I'm sorry that things are so difficult right now."

"I can't help but feel as if a lot of it is my fault," Elizabeth said as Bessie released her. "I should have dragged Andy along on our holiday with us, or maybe I just shouldn't have ended our relationship before I went. I wanted him to have a chance to see other women. I was arrogant enough to assume that in doing so he'd come to appreciate me even more."

"You need to stop worrying about the past and worry about the future," Bessie told her. "Do you want to help Andy with his decision or not?"

Elizabeth inhaled slowly, her eyes on the sea. "Yes," she said eventually. "Whatever else happens, even if we're never more than cordial acquaintances, I still want to help him. I genuinely think that I might be able to help, too. We talked so much about his hopes and dreams and what he wanted to accomplish with his restaurant that I feel as if I know what he needs at least as well as he does."

"So ring him back and agree to go and see the house."

"Besides that, he's terrible at making decisions," Elizabeth added. "He wants so badly to get everything just right that he never manages to actually do anything. Did you know that he's already written at least fifty different versions of what he wants to be his first menu? I've eaten hundreds of different dishes, all things he might want to put on the menu, but he could never actually finalise anything."

"If he needs anyone else to help with his selections, he's welcome to cook for me for days or weeks on end," Bessie told her.

Elizabeth laughed. "You'd be surprised how quickly you get tired of fancy meals all the time. That's especially true if you have the same chicken dish every day for a week with just tiny changes to the sauce, changes that you can't taste but that some people think are hugely significant."

"I think he needs to find a location before he worries about the menu," Bessie said.

"He does, and I'm going to have to help him. I'll ring him and see if he can arrange for us to see the house the day after tomorrow. I'll collect you around half nine, if that works for you and Andy and the estate agent."

Bessie nodded. "That's fine. Ring me if anything changes. Otherwise, I'll see you then."

"Now I just have to work up the nerve to ring Andy," Elizabeth said.

Bessie thought about offering to make the phone call herself, but bit her tongue. Elizabeth and Andy needed to work through their difficulties and the sooner they did that, the better.

"Just ring Andy," Elizabeth said firmly as she headed back towards the stairs. "Just ring Andy. Just ring Andy…"

Bessie and Andrew could hear her repeating the words to herself as she slowly climbed back up to her mansion home.

"She's still desperately in love with him, isn't she?" Andrew asked as Elizabeth disappeared from view.

"Yes, and I'm fairly certain he's still in love with her, too, in spite of his relationship with Jennifer. I haven't decided yet whether I think they should try their relationship again yet or not, though. Regardless, it would be good if they could find a way to work together again. Everyone on the island would benefit if Andy started catering events for Elizabeth again, and we all want Andy to open his restaurant, too."

Andrew nodded. "And now that we've had a short rest, shall we walk a bit farther?"

"I feel as if I want to walk forever. What I don't want to do is go back and read the case file again. It just feels futile."

"Do you want to talk about the case?"

Bessie frowned. "Not really, but we should. It's just frustrating because there is so little there to work with, and I can't help but feel as if something awful must have happened to Michelle and Dazaray."

Andrew nodded. "There's no sign of foul play, but there's really no sign of anything."

"Let's start at the beginning. According to Luke, Michelle and Dazaray had dinner with him on the tenth of July, which was a Wednesday. He claims that they left around seven o'clock to walk back to Michelle's parents' house, which was only a short distance away. Dazaray was in a pushchair, and the walk should have taken them about ten minutes, according to Sherry."

"Except they never arrived back at the house."

"Is it possible that they did go back to the house, but then went out again?" Bessie asked. "I can't remember if Michelle's parents were asked about that or not."

"I'm not certain, but it's an interesting question. Her parents were out that evening, which is one of the reasons why they assumed that Michelle had stayed with Luke."

"Because she didn't normally stay with him on a weeknight, but they thought she hadn't wanted to be home alone while they were out."

Andrew nodded. "Stanley and Jessica didn't get home until two in the morning. Michelle could have spent hours at home after her dinner with Luke before they arrived home."

"According to Sherry, at the time of the disappearance, the police went door to door, all along the route that Michelle would have taken from Luke's to her home. They failed to find anyone who had definitely seen her that evening. Many of the neighbours weren't at home at the right time, though, and most of the others probably would have been busy making dinner or doing other things."

Andrew nodded. "One woman did say that she thought she might have seen them, but she also admitted that she saw them walking up and down the street quite regularly and couldn't definitely say what time she'd seen them on that particular Wednesday."

"Michelle had also walked to Luke's earlier in the day. It's possible that the neighbour saw them going in that direction."

"Indeed."

"So we've no idea when Michelle and Dazaray disappeared. If Luke was involved in whatever happened to her, then he could be lying about them having dinner with him that evening. Working backwards, that would make the last time they were seen about midday on the tenth."

"Assuming that April is telling the truth."

Bessie sighed. "I thought it was quite sweet that April and

Michelle had lunch together every Wednesday whenever they could. I just wish they'd gone out for a meal somewhere instead of having lunch at Michelle's parents' house."

"If we keep working backwards, discounting April's statement, Michelle's parents both said that they spoke to her on the morning of the tenth before they left for work."

"Any of the witnesses could be lying, but I can't imagine they're all in it together," Bessie said. "Michelle must have been at home when her parents left for work that morning."

"We can go back a bit further and talk about the last known confirmed sighting of Michelle and Dazaray, though. Sherry has offered to send me a copy of the video recording from the grocery shop that captured them doing some shopping."

"I spent far too long just staring at the photograph that was taken from that video. It all just looks so ordinary, like an everyday trip to the shops. Dazaray looked a bit grumpy, and Michelle looked a bit stressed – exactly what you'd expect, really."

"Sherry has watched the video a number of times, and she doesn't think there is anything in it that will help with the investigation. From what she could see, Michelle doesn't speak to anyone in the shop, aside from the woman behind the till on her way out. You'll have read what she said when the police interviewed her."

"She said that she barely remembered the conversation, but that all of the customers were the same to her, really. She reckoned she'd said something about how cute Dazaray was and that Michelle said something about how high the prices were getting, and by that time she'd have had everything scanned and ready for Michelle to pay."

"It didn't help that she'd been working at that location for only a few weeks and hadn't had a chance to get to know any of the regular customers yet. Having said that, no one else at the shop seemed to have known Michelle well."

Bessie nodded. "I read all their statements. They all said the same thing, that they recognised her as a regular, but none of them could remember ever having had more than just a casual chat with her. One of the women said that Michelle was always busy with Dazaray, who was a handful. She said Michelle never had time to say anything much."

"That trip to the shops was on Tuesday afternoon. For what it's worth, Michelle did buy the ingredients for shepherd's pie, which is what April claims they ate on Wednesday."

"I found April quite believable. She seemed genuinely worried about her friend."

"She did," Andrew agreed.

"But then, I found all of the witnesses quite believable. Everyone seemed incredibly concerned. Her mother was nearly inconsolable in her first interview."

"I'm looking forward to getting updates from Sherry on where everyone is now. Maybe when Sherry goes back to talk to everyone the solution to the case will be obvious to her."

"We can hope."

"Was there anyone you didn't believe?" Andrew asked.

Bessie thought for a moment and then shook her head. "Luke seemed upset. Stanley seemed more angry than anything, but that may just have been frustration because he thought the police should be doing more."

"He made several remarks about how they were wasting their time talking to everyone when they should be out searching for Michelle and Dazaray."

"Except there simply wasn't anywhere to look," Bessie sighed. "As I said earlier, Jessica was very upset. She seemed particularly worried about Dazaray, but I suppose I can understand that. Dazaray was just a baby, really."

"And you've already said you believed April's story about seeing Michelle on Wednesday afternoon."

"I did, and the evidence from the house seemed to confirm her story. There was part of a shepherd's pie left in the refrigerator and dirty dishes in the dishwasher, which was consistent with two adults and a child having had lunch together that day."

"What about Krista?" Andrew asked.

"She claimed that she hadn't seen Michelle since the weekend before Michelle disappeared, but that they were supposed to be meeting on Friday to take their children to the park. As far as I could tell, she wasn't all that close to Michelle, but she did seem upset when she found out that she was missing. She seemed concerned that someone was kidnapping young women off the street and that she might be next."

"We haven't really come up with many questions for me to take back to Sherry."

"I think she needs to dig more deeply into all of the different relationships," Bessie said after a moment's thought. "According to Luke, he and Michelle were very happy together, and everyone else seemed to agree with him on the subject, but surely they had disagreements from time to time. I'd like Sherry to ask April and Krista about everything Michelle ever said about her relationship with Luke."

Andrew nodded. "I agree. Both women were mostly questioned about the last time they'd seen their friend. While they both said that, as far as they knew, Michelle and Luke were happy together, they weren't asked anything further."

"Michelle's parents had a bit more to say, but it was mostly about how wonderful they thought Luke was. I got the impression that they didn't care for Dylan, Dazaray's father."

"They were fairly careful about what they said, but I agree. Michelle's father, in particular, made several comments about how fortunate Michelle was to have Luke in her life now. I believe the words he used were that she'd 'traded up' from her former boyfriend."

Bessie frowned. "I think Sherry should also ask April and Krista about Michelle's relationship with her parents."

Andrew nodded. "It might be interesting to hear what they all have to say about one another, actually. We get bits of that in their interviews, but I'd like them all to be specifically questioned about everyone else."

Bessie opened her mouth to reply, but she was interrupted by a loud shriek.

"Aaaaabbbbbyyyyyyy," a voice shouted across the sand.

Bessie stopped and then smiled as Aalish Watterson raced across the sand towards them.

CHAPTER 8

Aalish flung herself into Bessie's arms and began to babble excitedly at her.

"Any idea what she's saying?" Bessie asked Andrew when the toddler stopped for a breath.

"None at all, but she's very cute," he replied,

"Aalish, you need to wait for Mummy," Grace said when she reached them a moment later. She put her hand on her stomach and took a few panting breaths.

"Are you okay?" Bessie asked as Aalish wiggled to get down.

"I'm fine, but this pregnancy is already slowing me down. Aalish, on the other hand, seems to get faster every day. I hate keeping her inside, but it's worrying, having her out here on the beach when I can't keep up with her. I'm terrified that she'll run into the sea one day."

Aalish was busy jumping up and down in a small tide pool nearby, splashing water everywhere.

"She's going to be covered in sand," Bessie said.

Grace nodded. "I'm used to that. At least she's stopped

trying to eat it all the time. Now she only eats it when she's hungry."

Bessie laughed. "Children are a great deal of work, aren't they?"

"They are," Andrew replied. "They're worth it, too, even on the most difficult of days."

Grace nodded and then rubbed her tummy. "We wouldn't be having another if we didn't love Aalish so desperately. I do think it might have been smart to wait a bit longer before we started trying for a second one, but there are advantages to having them close together, or so I hope."

"There are," Andrew assured her.

"You must make certain to take care of yourself," Bessie said. "Pregnancy is hard work, and so is looking after a toddler."

"I don't think I anticipated just how difficult it was going to be," Grace said with a sigh. "When we first started talking about having another child, Aalish wasn't even walking yet. Now she's running and climbing, and she's only going to get more active over the next six months, all while I get bigger and slower and tireder, which isn't even a word."

Bessie laughed. "There's nothing wrong with making up your own words."

"It didn't seem to do Shakespeare any harm," Andrew added.

"I really shouldn't complain. My mother has been coming up nearly every day to spend some time with Aalish, and Hugh does everything with her when he's home, but I was rather spoiled when I was expecting her. Looking back, I think I just slept and ate and very little else."

"If there's anything I can do, please let me know. You're always welcome to bring Aalish down to the beach by my cottage for a play. I'm not very fast, either, but at least you'd have another set of eyes keeping watch over her," Bessie offered.

"Thank you," Grace said. "I may take you up on that one day, but not during a cold case investigation."

"I could make time for you if you need me, but I do have a lot more time on my hands between cases," Bessie admitted.

Aalish suddenly stopped what she was doing and looked up the beach. "Daaaaaaaaa," she yelled before taking off running as fast as her little legs would carry her.

Grace started after her and then grinned when she spotted Hugh walking towards them.

"There's my girl," Hugh said as he swept Aalish up into his arms. "And my beautiful bride," he added, dropping a kiss on the top of Grace's head as he joined them.

"She's wearing me out," Grace told him.

He laughed. "It's a good thing I got home when I did, then. I'll take her inside and get her ready for her bath. You can chat with Bessie and Andrew for as long as you'd like."

Grace looked at Bessie and frowned. "I hope you won't think I'm being rude if I go inside with Hugh and Aalish."

"Not at all," Bessie said quickly. "We need to get back, anyway. It's getting late." She quickly hugged Grace and then Hugh, who was still holding Aalish. Aalish kindly rubbed a handful of sand into Bessie's hair while babbling loudly in her ear.

"They seem incredibly happy together," Andrew remarked as he and Bessie watched the little family walk back to their house on the beach.

"They do. I hope it lasts. I'm certain it must be hard work."

"It is, but it's worth the time and effort."

The pair turned around and began the long walk back to their cottages.

"I still miss her," Andrew said after a short while. "I don't think I truly understood how much I loved my wife until after she passed away."

"I'm sorry," Bessie said softly.

He took her hand and gave it a squeeze. "Thank you for being my friend," he said. "Our friendship is very important to me."

"It's important to me, too."

They walked the rest of the way in companionable silence. Back at Treoghe Bwaane, Andrew quickly checked that Bessie's cottage had been undisturbed while they'd been walking. Then he kissed Bessie on the cheek and made his way back to his own cottage. Bessie locked her doors and switched the ringer off on the telephone and then headed up to bed.

THE SUN WAS SHINING BRIGHTLY when she woke up just after six the next morning. After her shower, she patted on the rose-scented dusting powder that reminded her of Matthew Saunders. When she closed her eyes, she could almost picture the small bouquet of roses that he'd given her once.

"Marriage is difficult work," she said softly as she combed her hair. "Perhaps we wouldn't have succeeded at it."

Her heart insisted that she and Matthew would have been together forever, but it was impossible for Bessie to imagine the life that she would have had if Matthew had survived his ocean crossing.

"It would have been very different to this life," she said thoughtfully as she poured herself some cereal. "I'd have been in America, not here." As she ate her breakfast, she wondered how different the lives of her friends would have been if they'd never met her. A knock on the door shook Bessie out of her reverie.

"I woke up bright and early and decided that a walk on the beach was a better way to spend my time than going back to sleep," Andrew told her when she opened the door.

"Just let me put on my shoes," she replied. "I'm a bit behind today. I've been lost in thought, wondering how different everything would be if I'd married Matthew and moved back to America when I was eighteen."

Andrew frowned. "We'd never have met. I doubt very much this cold case unit would exist, which means a number of killers would still be walking around, unpunished."

Bessie nodded. "So many things would be different. It's probably best not to even think about it."

They walked to the stairs to Thie yn Traie and then turned around and walked back to Bessie's cottage.

"We've hours yet before Castle Rushen opens," Bessie said when they reached it. "Maybe I'll read the case file again."

"Maybe we should leave now and just wander around Castletown until the castle opens," Andrew suggested.

"That sounds as if it would be a good deal more fun than reading the case file again."

"I'll go and see if Matt is out of bed yet. If he isn't, I'll get him moving so we can leave as soon as possible."

Bessie let Andrew out and then stood in the kitchen, wondering what she should do next. *There's really no point in getting the case file out, not if we're going out soon. It would be much smarter to simply curl up with a good book.*

An hour later, when Andrew knocked on her door, Bessie was several chapters into the latest book in a series she'd been enjoying for years.

"That took longer than anticipated," Andrew said apologetically as Bessie let him and Matt into the cottage. "Helen rang, and then one of the grandsons needed some advice and, well, we're here now."

A few minutes later, they were on their way to Castletown.

"Tell me about the castle," Matt said from the back of the car as Andrew headed south.

"It's medieval," Bessie replied. "It was originally begun around 1200 and probably finished at some point in the 1600s. During the English Civil War, the Earl of Derby lived there for some years. It was there that his wife received word that he'd been executed. In later years, it was used as a prison, but now it's mostly a museum."

"And you'll be able to tell me what I'm seeing as we go around it?" he asked.

"I can, but there are very helpful signs just about everywhere inside the castle. They explain its history far better than I ever could. Each room has a sign showing how the room was used at different times in the past," Bessie told him.

"I was never very interested in history when I was younger, but the older I get, the more I find myself fascinated by it," Matt said.

"I'm the same," Andrew said. "And the island's history is particularly interesting."

Andrew parked his car in the small car park near the museum. There was just enough time for a short stroll through the town before the museum opened for the day.

"That was better than I'd been expecting," Matt said when they exited the castle ninety minutes later. "I almost asked if we could do it all again, but I know you two have a meeting later."

Bessie nodded. "But we could come back another day."

Matt thought for a moment and then shrugged. "Maybe not this trip, but if I ever come over with my father again, I'd love to go around the castle a second time."

"In the meantime, you can read all about it," Andrew said,

gesturing towards the small bag of books that Matt was carrying.

He laughed. "I hadn't planned on buying a half-dozen books on the island's history and historical sites, but I couldn't seem to stop myself."

"I think you'll enjoy the books you selected," Bessie told him. "They're all favourites of mine."

The trio had lunch at a small pub near the castle before they walked back to Andrew's car for the journey back to Laxey.

"Peel Castle tomorrow?" Matt asked as Andrew started to drive.

"Unfortunately, I have plans for tomorrow morning," Bessie said. "But you and your father can visit Peel Castle without me."

"I don't mind waiting for another day," Matt replied. "I'm afraid I was rather spoiled today, having you along to elaborate on various points and help me spot the most interesting things in every room. Now I want the same expert tour at Peel Castle."

Bessie laughed. "But there's an audio tour at Peel Castle. You don't need me."

"Bessie knows a good deal more than the audio tour shares," Andrew said. "You can spend tomorrow reading all of your new books, and we can visit Peel Castle later in the week."

"Perfect," Matt said.

They got back to Laxey with just enough time for Bessie to comb her hair and change her shoes before they needed to leave for Ramsey. Andrew chuckled as he joined the main road.

"What's so funny?" Bessie asked.

"Charles is in the car behind us, and I believe Harry is in the car behind him."

The three cars pulled into the Seaview's car park one right after the other. Bessie and Andrew got out of his car and waited for the others.

"We really should arrange things so that we don't all have to drive," Andrew said as Harry and Charles walked towards them.

"I'm going to Douglas after the meeting," Harry said. "I have an appointment with the Chief Constable."

"And I'm going to Peel to talk to an inspector and a few constables about missing person cases," Charles said. "Now that everyone on the island knows about the cold case unit, everyone wants to talk to us."

Andrew frowned. "I'm sorry. Perhaps we shouldn't have given Dan Ross an interview."

"At least he's not still creeping around, trying to work out what we're doing here," Harry said. "And I don't mind talking to the Chief Constable or anyone else, really, not as long as I have plenty of time to work on our case. In this instance, I didn't need all that much time. There wasn't much in the case file with which to work."

Charles nodded. "There wasn't very much there, and I'm used to missing person cases having less than murder investigations."

The little group walked into the hotel together. Bessie waved at Sandra, who was behind the reception desk.

"You're in the penthouse again," she told them. "But it's just biscuits today."

The look on Sandra's face made Bessie stop and cross to the desk. "What's wrong?" she asked.

Sandra made a face. "Nothing, really, except the chef and the pastry chef are at war with one another, which was lovely when they were battling over tarts, because they made hundreds and hundreds of them, and we all got to take some home. It's not lovely now, though, as Chef has declared that he won't make another sweet thing ever again unless Jasper gets rid of the pastry chef, and the pastry chef is now insisting that he can't work in a hostile environment and has gone off somewhere, angry. Jasper is trying to work out how to manage dinner if we don't have any puddings, and Stuart is threatening to get rid of Chef and the pastry chef and shut the restaurant for a month until replacements can be found."

"Oh dear," Bessie said. "We'll enjoy our biscuits and not complain."

"They're shop-bought," Sandra warned her. "It was the best we could do under the circumstances."

"I'm sure they'll be fine. We're here to work, really."

Sandra nodded. "I hope you find the killer if it's a murder investigation."

Bessie smiled. "I can't talk about the case, but thank you." She walked over to Andrew, who had waited for her.

"Just biscuits?" Andrew asked when they were on the lift.

Bessie explained what had happened, finishing as the lift doors opened on the building's top floor. They walked to the conference room and went inside. Everyone else was already sitting around the table. Andrew quickly poured himself a cup of coffee and put a few biscuits on a plate. Bessie did the same but opted for tea. As soon as they sat down, Andrew began.

"I know there isn't a lot to work with here, but we need to get back to Sherry with questions. Where do you want to start?" he asked.

"Clearly, the woman and her child have met with foul play," Harry said. "Sherry needs to question them with that in mind."

"Not necessarily," Bessie said. "It's possible that Michelle disappeared of her own accord."

"If she'd done that, she'd have stayed in touch with her

parents," Doona argued. "She wouldn't have wanted them worrying about her for all these years."

"Maybe they aren't worried," Hugh said. "It doesn't sound as if anyone has been questioned on the case in nine years. Maybe Michelle came back and is living happily with Luke or her parents again."

Andrew shook his head. "Sherry hasn't spoken to the various witnesses in the case yet, but she has done some investigative work. Michelle and Dazaray are still missing."

"So they were either taken by a stranger, or one of the witnesses knows more than he or she is admitting," Harry said. "Sherry needs to look at local sex offenders and see if she can find out if any from outside the area may have been in Dover at the right time."

Andrew nodded. "Some work was done in that area when Michelle and Dazaray originally disappeared, but not enough, in my opinion."

"She should see if anyone on the list who lived in Dover at the time has since moved away," John added.

"I think Sherry needs to find out more about the relationships between the various witnesses," Bessie said. "Michelle's parents seemed very fond of Luke. Maybe that put pressure on her to stay in the relationship even if she was unhappy with him."

"From what I read, the focus needs to be on finding someone outside of the limited number of witnesses that were initially identified," Charles said. "I want to know more about Michelle. How likely would she have been to trust a stranger? What about someone she recognised from the neighbourhood but didn't really know? What about Dazaray? Did she sometimes run ahead of her mother when they walked? Luke said she was in her pushchair when they left his house, but what if Michelle let her out and Dazaray ran into a neighbour's house? I'm fairly certain Michelle would have followed her."

Andrew was busy scribbling notes. Eventually, he looked up. "Anyone else?"

"I'm more suspicious of the people who knew her," Hugh said. "Actually, I'm just suspicious of Luke, but I don't know why. There was something in his interview that bothered me."

"Something?" Charles repeated.

Hugh flushed. "I'm sorry. I've read the interview at least a dozen times, but I can't quite work out what's bothering me. I really want to get on a ferry and then drive down to Dover and talk to the man myself. He may be exactly what he seems to be, but I'd really like to meet him."

Bessie swallowed a sigh. She loved working with the cold case unit, but she shared Hugh's frustration.

"Does anyone have anything else?" Andrew asked.

"It seems to me that there are several different possibilities, and they each need a very different approach," John said. "If Michelle disappeared voluntarily, then Sherry needs to talk to her family and friends. It's likely that one of them helped her. Disappearing, especially with a small child, isn't easy."

"She needs to question them anyway, because one or more of them could have had something to do with any foul play that may have taken place," Harry said.

"But I think she'd do better to focus her attention on someone outside of Michelle's small group of family and friends," Charles said.

The conversation continued to go around in circles for several minutes. Eventually, Andrew held up his hand.

"There are clearly several different possibilities for what happened to Michelle and Dazaray. I'll pass along everything we've discussed to Sherry, and we'll meet again the day after tomorrow, once she's had a chance to interview everyone again," he said. "Obviously, you know how to reach me if you have any other questions or concerns between now and then."

After a few more minutes of conversation, people slowly began to pack up their things. As usual, Harry and Charles were the first to leave. The others weren't far behind, though. Jasper was standing in the corridor as Bessie and Andrew walked out of the room.

"I'm sorry it was just biscuits and tea," he said.

Bessie pulled him into a hug. "You look stressed," she told him.

"I'm better now than I was an hour ago. Chef and I have reached a shaky and, no doubt, very temporary truce. It will be fine, eventually, but I'm about to head down to the bar and have a drink or two. I just wanted to apologise to you before I started drinking."

"We are only paying for biscuits. We've no right to expect anything other than biscuits," Andrew reminded him.

"Yes, I know, but I do like to spoil you all a bit. You're doing very important work here," Jasper replied.

He walked with them to the front of the hotel and then gave Bessie another hug.

"We'll have something nicer for you the next time you meet, even if I have to drive to a bakery somewhere and buy it myself," he promised.

CHAPTER 9

"Ready to go and visit Patrick?" Andrew asked as they walked out of the hotel.

"I'm not looking forward to it," Bessie admitted.

"It's difficult seeing old friends struggling."

The drive into Douglas seemed to go more quickly than normal. Bessie gave Andrew directions to the care home where Patrick was staying. There was only a small car park outside, but Andrew was able to find a space.

"Do you want me to come in or wait here?" he asked.

"Oh, come in, please. I may well be as much a stranger to Patrick as you are, and he may be more willing to talk to another man than to me."

The woman behind the desk in the small lobby smiled at them as they walked inside.

"Good afternoon. How can we help you today?"

"We're hoping to visit Patrick Lace," Bessie replied.

She nodded. "I'm sure he'd welcome visitors, but you should be aware that he doesn't always remember his friends or family members," the woman told them. "I don't want you to be disappointed when you see him."

"We understand," Bessie said.

"I'll just get someone to take you through, then." She pushed a button on the desk in front of her. After a moment, the door behind her opened and a brunette in her mid-thirties walked out.

"Aunt Bessie? What brings you here?" she asked.

"Susan Harrison? I didn't realise you were working here now," Bessie replied.

"I've been here for only about three months. After my maternity leave, I decided to look for a new job closer to home," Susan explained.

"And how is the baby?" Bessie asked.

"Not a baby any longer, really. He's two, and he goes to nursery while I'm here. He loves it there. For whatever reason, most of his age group is other little boys, and they have far too much fun chasing each other around and creating chaos for the poor staff."

Bessie laughed. "How nice for him, though."

"Who are you here to see?"

"Patrick Lace."

Susan frowned. "Do you know him well?"

"Not really. I know his mother somewhat better."

"I'll just warn you that Patrick has some problems with his memory. He has good days and bad days, though. He's in good spirits today, at least."

"That's good to hear."

"He's in the conservatory at the back of the house. I'll just take you back." Susan turned around and waited for Bessie and Andrew to follow her through the door. Then she led them down a short corridor before they turned and walked down a longer one. The door at the end of the hall opened into a small conservatory. Two men were sitting on opposite sides of the room. Both were reading paperback books.

"Patrick? Aunt Bessie has come for a visit," Susan said brightly.

One of the men looked up and smiled, a slightly confused look on his face. "Aunt Bessie? Oh, of course. Bessie Cubbon. How are you?"

"I'm very well, thank you. How are you?" Bessie replied as she sat down next to him. Andrew sat on the other side of Patrick.

Patrick shrugged. "I'm getting older, so much so that I've had to come and live here instead of at home. It isn't too bad here, though. The food is good, and I never have to do the washing-up."

Bessie laughed. "That sounds quite nice."

"I do forget things quite a lot, but as long as I don't forget which room is mine, I suppose the rest doesn't really matter," Patrick told her.

"I should introduce you to my friend," Bessie said. "This is Andrew Cheatham."

"Oh, from the cold case unit? When the article about it was in the paper, we all talked about it for ages. It's very nice to meet you," Patrick told Andrew.

"It's nice to meet you, too," Andrew replied.

"But you didn't just come to say hello, especially not if you brought a police inspector with you. What's happened? Has someone been murdered? I can't recall ever being involved in a murder investigation, but maybe I've forgotten. Am I a part of your most recent cold case?"

Bessie shook her head. "Not at all. Nothing has happened, although I did wonder if you had a new telephone number for your mother."

Patrick stared at her for a moment and then slowly recited the number that Bessie had for Hazel.

"That's always been her telephone number. Always. It's one of the few things I can remember clearly."

"Does she visit often?" Bessie asked.

Patrick frowned. "I don't know. Maybe. Probably. She would, wouldn't she?"

"What about Laura and Delores?"

Patrick shrugged. "I keep hoping that Margaret will visit. I haven't seen her in such a very long time. And Paul. It would be nice to see Paul again."

Bessie nodded. "If you see your mother, please tell her that I was asking about her."

"Yes, of course. I'm sorry, I've forgotten your name."

Bessie patted his arm. "It doesn't matter. What would you like to talk about?"

"Cricket," Patrick replied.

Bessie looked at Andrew, hoping he could help. She knew next to nothing about cricket.

Andrew and Patrick chatted about batsmen and bowlers while Bessie sat back and pretended to listen. After half an hour, Patrick sighed.

"Is it nearly time for dinner? I'm getting very hungry."

"It is, yes," Susan said as she stuck her head into the room. "You can make your way to the dining room whenever you're ready."

"I'm ready now," Patrick said quickly.

"That makes two of us," the other man said. He carefully tucked a bookmark into his book and then slowly got to his feet.

Patrick stood up. "It was nice talking to you," he said as he rushed towards the door.

Bessie hid a smile. Clearly, Patrick was eager to get in front of the other man, who was moving considerably slower.

"They aren't going to run out of food," the man muttered as he followed Patrick out of the room.

"That ended rather abruptly," Andrew said with a laugh.

"All of our residents love the food here," Susan said. "We all do, actually. I hope you enjoyed your time with Patrick."

"It was lovely, although not especially helpful," Bessie replied.

"I heard you asking about his visitors. He doesn't get many," Susan told her.

"Do you know when his mother last visited?" Bessie asked.

"I don't, sorry. We don't keep track of visitors unless we have to because of disagreements or issues. I can tell you that she hasn't visited him while I've been here, and I'm here five days a week from eight to six."

Bessie frowned. "What about his daughters, Laura and Delores?"

"I didn't even know he has daughters, and before you ask, I've never met Paul or Margaret, either."

"Paul was Patrick's brother, but he passed away years ago. Margaret was his wife, but she's been gone for a long time, too," Bessie explained.

Susan nodded. "Patrick's only consistent visitor is a friend called John. He comes to see Patrick at least once a week. I believe they went to primary school together."

"I'm glad he has someone who visits," Bessie said.

"We have a small group of volunteers who come in just to talk to our residents as well. Most of them are retired men and women who enjoy the conversations as much as our residents do. Every resident gets a visitor at least twice a week."

Bessie smiled. "How lovely."

"Perhaps you could ring Bessie if anyone from Patrick's family does come to see him," Andrew suggested. "You don't need to ring while they're here or anything, but it might be helpful to know if someone has been in."

Susan nodded. "I can do that. I can ask the other nurses to do the same, too."

Andrew shrugged. "If it isn't too much bother."

"It's no bother at all. I once spent an entire weekend sobbing in Aunt Bessie's spare bedroom because Phillip Williams broke up with me the day before my birthday. My parents couldn't hide how delighted they were because they didn't care for Phillip. Aunt Bessie was kind enough not to point out that I was only seventeen and had my entire life ahead of me. She just let me cry it out and then baked me a birthday cake. I've never forgotten her kindness."

Bessie blushed. "I'm glad I was able to help. Whatever happened to Phillip Williams?"

Susan laughed. "He married one of my friends, the one he'd ended things with me for, actually. The marriage only lasted about a year because he cheated on her. As much as I hate to admit it, my parents were right about him."

"I hate to ask, but is there any way you can look to see who is listed as Patrick's emergency contact? Don't do anything that could get you into any trouble," Bessie said.

"I can check, but I can't give out any telephone numbers or anything," Susan replied.

"That's fine. I'm just curious whether he's given you information for one of his daughters," Bessie told her.

"I'll go and take a quick look. You can wait here if you want."

"If the information is there, we can request it through the proper channels," Andrew told Bessie as Susan left the room.

She frowned. "I'd rather not involve the police, but I am starting to get a bit concerned about Hazel."

Andrew nodded. "Let's see what Susan finds."

The woman returned a few minutes later. "I'm sorry, but

the only name listed on his records is his mother's. The number we have is the same one that he told you when you were talking earlier."

Bessie sighed. "Thank you for trying."

"I can't help but wonder what's wrong," Susan said as she began to escort them through the building. "This is the first time we've had the police here since I've been working here."

"I'm retired," Andrew said quickly.

"But now you run the cold case unit that everyone is talking about all over the island. I suppose you can't tell me if Patrick is involved in one of your cold cases."

"I couldn't if he was, but he isn't," Bessie replied. "I rang his mother the other day and couldn't reach her. I'm simply trying to track her down."

"She isn't at home? I know Patrick told me that she doesn't go out very much these days."

"I've been to the house. She wasn't at home," Bessie explained.

Susan shrugged. "You should try visiting again. It's possible she forgot to pay her phone bill. Maybe she decided to just get a mobile phone. Maybe she's in hospital or has moved into a care home and we simply haven't been notified yet. We would have heard if she'd passed away."

Bessie nodded. "Thank you so much for your time today."

"I'm always happy to see you," Susan laughed. "I'll be forever grateful that you didn't let me ring Phillip and beg him to give me another chance. I could have ended up being the one who was cheated on instead of being married to the most wonderful man in the world."

"I'm glad you're so happy."

Susan laughed. "He's not really the most wonderful man in the world, but he's a great guy and he does his best to spoil me. More importantly, he's an amazing father to our little guy."

They'd reached the small foyer again. Susan gave Bessie a quick smile and then reached into her pocket and pulled out a small photo album. "This is my guy, and this is my little guy," she said, showing Bessie a wedding picture and then a photo of a grinning toddler.

"He's very handsome," Bessie said.

"Which one?" Susan asked.

Bessie laughed. "Both of them, of course."

As they walked back to Andrew's car, Bessie sighed.

"Do you think we should ring the police?" she asked as Andrew opened her door for her.

"Maybe we should do as Susan suggested and see if Hazel is at home now."

Bessie nodded. "I suppose it's possible that Hazel forgot to pay her telephone bill. Or maybe there's some sort of problem with the line about which she knows nothing. Of course, she wasn't home when we went around the house. And perhaps Esther has just missed her when she's been to the house as well."

"How many times has Esther been to the house?"

"She told me that she's been driving past it whenever she's out and that she went to the door at least once, but no one was home."

Andrew started the car. "Why don't we get something to eat first? I think Hazel is more likely to be home later in the evening."

Bessie nodded. "I'm worried, but I'm also hungry."

"Where would you like to go?"

She thought for a minute. "Actually, there used to be a lovely little café very near Hazel's house. I'm not even certain that it's still there, but they used to have wonderful food and even better puddings. It's the sort of place that Hazel might pop into occasionally, too."

"In that case, let's go and see if it's still there."

It didn't take them long to drive to the café. Bessie was delighted to see that it was still in business.

"It doesn't look as if they've done anything to the place since the last time I was here," she said as Andrew parked the car. "I hope they still have the same menu and kitchen staff."

The interior of the restaurant felt a bit tired, but everything was spotlessly clean.

"Sit anywhere," the young woman behind the counter told them as they walked in. "I'll be with you in a moment."

Bessie chose a table near the windows.

"We can almost see Hazel's house from here," Andrew said as he sat down opposite her.

"That's what I was thinking, but the road curves just a little too much."

Andrew nodded. "Do you know what sort of car she drives?"

"I believe she stopped driving years ago. I'm fairly certain she no longer owns a car."

"So she might come here for a meal once in a while because it's within walking distance of home."

"That's what I was thinking."

"Hello. How are you? Welcome to Sunny's Corner. I'm Sunny. We're happy to have you here," the woman said as she approached their table.

"Sunny's Corner?" Bessie echoed.

The other woman nodded. "We've only just changed the name, and we haven't had a chance to change the sign yet. We only just bought the café a few months ago."

Bessie did her best to hide her disappointment. "I didn't realise," she said. "Have you made many changes to the menu?"

"We've changed it completely," Sunny said. "Everything on our menu is either vegetarian or vegan." She handed them each a neatly printed and photocopied sheet. "I'm happy to answer any questions you might have about the menu."

Bessie looked at the sheet and then at Andrew. "They've changed the menu," she said.

He nodded. "One of my favourite restaurants in London is vegetarian. I'm happy to stay if you are."

Bessie read down the list of sandwiches, salads, and other offerings. "There's plenty on here that I'll eat," she said.

"Can I get you something to drink while you're looking over the menu?" Sunny asked. "We have a range of herbal teas as well as a variety of different sparkling waters."

Bessie read through the list of teas and chose one almost at random. Herbal hibiscus and honey sounded quite soothing, really. Andrew asked for coffee. When the woman returned with their drinks, they ordered.

"Do you have a pudding menu?" Bessie asked hopefully.

Sunny nodded. "I make a number of different vegetarian and vegan fairy cakes every day. I'll check what we have left when I'm in the kitchen."

"Chocolate is vegetarian, isn't it?" Bessie asked Andrew.

He nodded. "The vegetarian restaurant I go to in London does delicious chocolate biscuits. Sometimes I go in and just get a dozen or so to go."

When Sunny returned with their meals, she smiled at Bessie. "We have chocolate, vanilla, and strawberry fairy cakes for pudding tonight."

"Save a chocolate one for me," Bessie said quickly.

"I'll have one of each," Andrew said. "You can taste all of them if you'd like," he told Bessie.

"We'll see," Bessie replied as she picked up her fork. "I may be too full to eat more than the one fairy cake I ordered."

"This is surprisingly good," Bessie said after a few bites.

Andrew nodded. "It's better than I was expecting."

Sunny cleared their table and then brought out their pudding. As she put Bessie's plate in front of her, Bessie caught her eye.

"I have a friend who lives quite near here. I wonder if she's had an opportunity to try your food yet," she said, trying to sound casual.

"A few of our neighbours have been very supportive," Sunny replied. "There are a few who aren't very happy about the new menu, though, too."

Bessie nodded. "People can be very resistant to change. I can't see my friend Hazel minding, though. She's always enjoyed good food, and everything I had tonight was very good."

"Thank you."

"Have you met Hazel?" Bessie asked. "She's an older woman with grey hair and glasses, which probably describes nearly all of your neighbours."

Sunny laughed. "The neighbourhood is a mix of older residents who have been here for decades and young families who've either inherited the homes or bought them when the original owners passed away. I don't recall meeting anyone named Hazel, but our customers don't often introduce themselves."

Bessie nodded. "In that case, I shall be certain to tell her how much I enjoyed dinner here tonight. As I said, she lives quite nearby. I hope she'll become a regular customer for you."

"Thank you again."

"The fairy cakes aren't very large," Andrew said as Sunny walked away. "I'm very glad I got three of them. Would you like to share the vanilla and strawberry ones?"

"I'll have a quarter or so of each, if you don't mind," Bessie told him. "I have just enough room for one and a half fairy cakes."

Andrew chuckled and then carefully cut two of the cakes into pieces.

"They were all wonderful," Bessie told Sunny when she came to collect their empty plates.

"I'm so glad you enjoyed them. I'll keep an eye out for your friend."

"Thank you," Bessie replied.

Andrew paid for dinner, then the pair made their way out to the car.

"Of course, there's nowhere to park near Hazel's," Bessie said with a sigh as Andrew drove down the street.

"There's a light on inside the house," Andrew pointed out. "I can keep driving up and down until a space opens up, or I can let you out and you can go and knock."

Bessie thought for a moment. "It's getting late. It's entirely possible that none of these cars are going to get moved until morning. Just let me out and I'll go and see if Hazel is at home. As you say, there is a light on inside the house. That's a promising sign."

Andrew turned around and then drove down the street again. This time he stopped in the road right outside of Hazel's house. Bessie opened the door and got out of the car. Another car pulled up behind Andrew before she'd gone far. As he slowly drove away, Bessie walked up to Hazel's door. She knocked and then stepped back and slowly counted to one hundred before knocking again.

A moment later, the door swung open. The man on the doorstep appeared to be in his mid-forties. His hair was black and his eyes were dark. He glared at Bessie.

"What do you want?" he demanded angrily.

CHAPTER 10

Bessie gasped and took a step backwards. The man frowned.

"You're too old to be selling anything," he snapped.

"I came to see Hazel," Bessie said, working hard to keep her voice from shaking.

He stared at her for a moment, clearly thinking about how to respond. "She's in bed," he said eventually. "She's old, too. She goes to bed early."

"Who are you?" Bessie asked.

"That's none of your business."

"Hazel is a dear friend of mine. I'm worried about her."

"She's fine. She's being well looked after. Good night."

As the man started to shut the door, Bessie pushed her foot forwards to stop it. It was a move she immediately regretted as she watched the man's face turn red. There was a long and incredibly awkward pause before he inhaled very slowly.

"I can ring the police and have you arrested," he said tightly, clearly struggling to keep his anger in check.

"That won't be necessary." Andrew's voice came from behind Bessie.

She turned and gave him a grateful smile. He reached the doorstep and put his arm around Bessie.

"Good evening," he said, slipping his foot over the threshold. Bessie slowly moved her foot back.

The man inside the house sighed. "Go away," he said.

"We've been quite concerned about Hazel," Andrew told him. "We'd appreciate an opportunity to speak to her."

"Like I just told the old lady, she's in bed. She doesn't always sleep well, so she goes to bed nice and early. I'm not going to wake her up because a couple of random strangers turn up on her doorstep."

Andrew nodded. "We'll leave a message for her, then. Please ask her to ring Elizabeth Cubbon at her earliest convenience."

The man shrugged. "If I remember. We're about to go, actually. If you'd been a few minutes later, no one would have answered your knock."

"Perhaps you could leave Hazel a note," Andrew suggested.

"Maybe." The man took a step back. "I'm closing the door now."

Andrew nodded and moved his foot out of the way. Bessie sighed as the door shut loudly.

"Are you okay?" Andrew asked as they reached the pavement and turned left.

"I think so. I behaved rather foolishly."

"You're concerned about your friend, and finding that gentleman in her home isn't terribly reassuring."

Andrew stopped when they reached the corner. "If you truly are okay, it might be best if you wait here."

"Wait here?" Bessie echoed, looking back down the street at Hazel's house.

He nodded. "He said, 'We're about to go.' If that's true, he and whoever else was at the house with him may be just about to leave. I'd like to try to follow them if we can."

"So you want me to stay here and watch the house."

"Exactly. You can stand in the doorway of the shop here and be almost totally out of sight."

Bessie looked at the doorway and sighed. "I'm almost certain there are spiders in there."

"You don't care for spiders?"

"Not hanging above my head in the dark."

Andrew chuckled. "You can stand right here on the corner if you'd rather, but anyone walking out of Hazel's house would be certain to see you."

Bessie looked back down the street and then took a few steps closer to the dark doorway. She looked up at the overhanging roof and frowned at the cobwebs she could see. "You're going to get the car?" she asked.

"As quickly as I can," he promised.

"I'll be here."

Andrew nodded and walked briskly away. Bessie stood close to the building, just a step away from the recessed doorway. With nothing else to do, she began counting slowly. At three hundred ninety-six, she heard the sound of a door opening.

As she stepped under the overhang into the doorway, she saw the angry man walk out of Hazel's house. The woman behind him stopped to lock the door. They walked down the steps and the pavement and then turned right. Bessie blew out a breath she hadn't realised she'd been holding.

She jumped when a car suddenly honked its horn. The couple in front of her stopped and turned around, giving Bessie a good look at the woman. The man said something to her and then they continued on their way. A car rolled to a stop in front of Bessie. She waited until the couple turned the corner and then rushed over and jumped into Andrew's car.

"I think the woman is Delores," Bessie said as Andrew pulled away from the kerb.

He nodded. "I honked when I saw them walk under the streetlight."

"That was very clever of you."

He glanced at her and laughed. "I may have done this sort of thing before."

Bessie flushed. "Yes, of course."

When they turned the corner, there was no sign of the couple.

"They may well be in one of the cars, just about to pull out," Andrew said. "I'm going to wait here for a moment."

As he finished speaking, a car about halfway down the street suddenly came to life. The driver reversed and then pulled forwards quickly, out into the street.

"We're going to look suspicious very quickly on these residential roads," Andrew said. "We may not be able to follow them far. Make a note of the number plate if you can."

Bessie dug into her handbag for a small notebook and a pen. As the car in front of them stopped at a light, Andrew drove up behind them.

"I got it," she said happily after writing down the number plate.

"Excellent. I'm going to turn left here and then try to circle around and get behind them again. I don't think they've noticed us, and I'd like to keep it that way."

As the car in front went straight on, Andrew turned left and then quickly turned left and left again. When they turned back on to the first road again, they could just see taillights in the distance.

"That should be them, shouldn't it?" Bessie asked.

"I believe so. We'll follow for a bit from a distance."

A moment later, the car in front turned on to a busier road. Andrew waited to follow until another car got between their car and the one with the couple.

"Do your best to keep them in sight," he told Bessie. "It's highly likely that we'll lose them somewhere, but maybe we'll learn something along the way."

"We're heading towards Ramsey," Bessie said after a few minutes.

Andrew nodded. "I just hope the car between us is going to stay with us. I'd rather we not be spotted."

The three cars crossed the mountain together, with Andrew hanging back and just keeping the first car in sight. It wasn't until they were nearly at the Ramsey Hairpin that he sped up until he was right behind the second car.

"The car in front is turning left," Bessie said as they made their way into Ramsey.

Andrew frowned. "I hope we won't be too obvious if we follow them."

As the car that had been between them drove off, Andrew indicated and then followed the first car into a small housing estate. He drove slowly, letting the first car speed into the estate and then turn right.

"What now?" Bessie asked as Andrew stopped the car.

"I'm hoping this is the only way in or out of the housing estate," he replied. "We'll stay here for a minute and then drive up and down the streets and see if we can see the car parked anywhere."

After a minute, Andrew drove to where the other car had turned. He slowly followed.

"Isn't that it?" Bessie asked a few seconds later.

"It is." Andrew stopped the car.

Bessie took a good look at the house. "It's badly in need of some attention."

"I'll just make a note of the address and then we'll go

home." Andrew pulled out a small notebook and pen. He was writing in the notebook as the front door of the house suddenly swung open. The same man who'd opened Hazel's door walked out and headed towards his car.

Bessie froze as the man appeared to notice them. Before he could react, Andrew started back down the road. Bessie couldn't stop herself from watching the man as they drove away. He simply stared after them.

Andrew and Bessie were silent as he drove them out of the estate and then turned towards Laxey.

"I'm going to have John find out who owns the house and the car," Andrew said eventually.

"As I said, I think the woman with him was Delores. It's been years since the last time I saw her, though."

"From their body language, I'd say they are a couple. Didn't you tell me that Delores has been married multiple times?"

"She has. If I really try, I might be able to remember exactly how many. It's either three or four, I believe, although I suppose it's possible that she's recently remarried."

"I'll send everything we know in an email to John before I go to bed," Andrew said as he pulled into the parking area outside of Bessie's cottage. "What are your plans for tomorrow?"

"I'm going to look at Hilary Christian's house with Andy and Elizabeth. He values her opinion and she's – well – she's desperate to see him, even if she can't admit that to anyone, including herself."

Andrew laughed. "I really hope those two end up together one day. They seem perfect for one another, in spite of everything that's happened."

"I'm not certain Elizabeth will ever be able to forgive Andy for believing horrible things about her."

"Andy was, well, let's say naïve. He's simply not accustomed to having money and, therefore, being a target for fortune hunters. I don't expect he'll make the same mistake again."

"I should hope not. What are your plans for tomorrow?"

"Matthew and I were talking about driving up to the Point of Ayre so he can have a look at the island's northernmost point. Is there anywhere between here and there to get lunch?"

"There used to be a nice café in Bride. I'm not certain it's still there, but I can give you directions. Why don't you come in for a cuppa?"

Andrew glanced at his watch and then nodded. "It isn't as late as I thought it was. I will, thank you."

Over tea and biscuits, they talked about Hazel and Delores before Bessie gave Andrew directions to the café in Bride.

"I'll collect you at half one for the unit meeting," he told her as she let him out.

"Thank you. I'll see you tomorrow," Bessie replied. She shut and locked the door behind him and then checked that all of her doors and windows were shut and locked. After switching off the ringer on the telephone, Bessie headed up to bed.

∼

BESSIE WAS PACING NERVOUSLY the next morning when someone knocked on her door.

"Elizabeth, good morning," she said, giving the young woman a hug.

"Is it?" Elizabeth asked. "It doesn't feel at all good. I'm really sorry that I agreed to do this. Maybe I should ring Andy and cancel. Better yet, maybe you could ring Andy and cancel."

"Or we could just go," Bessie suggested.

Elizabeth sighed. "Is the house nice?"

"It's very nice. I believe Andy was considering turning a large part of the ground floor into a restaurant with a large kitchen and then putting a small private kitchen on the first floor for his own personal use."

"So he'd live above his restaurant. I'm not certain that's ideal, but there would certainly be some benefits."

Bessie locked the door to her cottage and then followed Elizabeth to the young woman's fancy sports car. A moment later, they were on their way to Lonan.

"You're going to have to give me directions," Elizabeth said as they went. "I read the directions on the listing at least a dozen times, but I'm still not certain where I'm going."

"The turning is difficult to find from the road. It's not much of a road at first, too, but it does get better quite quickly."

A few minutes later, Bessie told her to slow down. "It's just here," she said, pointing.

"Here? That's not a road, it's a clearing."

"Trust me, that's it."

Elizabeth indicated and then slowly inched her way on to what appeared to be a dirt road. "Before Andy can do anything with the house, he's going to have to do a lot of work out here," she commented. "People need to be able to find the restaurant, and they aren't going to want to have to drive through mud and dirt to get there."

"He'll probably have to add some lighting. The road is difficult to find in daylight. I can't imagine how Hilary finds it after dark."

After a short distance, the road improved, and as they drove around a corner, Elizabeth gasped.

"What a beautiful property," she said.

"It is lovely," Bessie agreed.

THE KELLER FILE

"There's plenty of room out here for a large car park," Elizabeth said as she pulled up next to the other car that was parked in front of the house.

"Ready?" Bessie asked.

"No, but that isn't Andy's car. It must belong to the estate agent. Maybe we can get him or her to take us around the house quickly before Andy even gets here."

Bessie laughed as Elizabeth jumped out of the car and rushed towards the door. She followed more slowly, reaching the door as it swung open.

"Hello," Andy said, glancing at Elizabeth and then smiling broadly at Bessie. "Thanks for coming."

"I didn't see your car," Elizabeth blurted out.

"The estate agent drove," he explained as he stepped backwards to let them into the house.

They stepped inside and Elizabeth looked around the huge foyer.

"This is beautiful," she said after a moment. "You could put some lovely couches and chairs in this space, with a small bar along the back wall. People could have a drink while they wait for their table."

"I hadn't thought of that, but it would work," Andy replied.

"Ah, everyone is here." The dark-haired woman who walked into the room was a stranger to Bessie.

Andrew performed the introductions. "Bessie and Elizabeth, this is Sierra Montgomery."

"It's nice to meet you," Bessie said. "Have you been on the island for long?"

Sierra laughed. "What makes you think I wasn't born here?" she asked.

"I thought I knew all of the island's estate agents," Bessie replied. "Of course, it's possible that you've lived here for

121

your entire life and only recently became an estate agent. You've no need to answer if you think I'm being nosy."

"Oh, not at all. We moved to the island six months ago. My husband works for one of the insurance companies. I stayed home with the kids for as long as I could stand it and then decided to go back to work. The good thing about being an estate agent is that my hours are fairly flexible," she explained.

"How are you finding the island?" Bessie asked.

"So far, I love it here, but I do miss the shopping back in Manchester."

"You need a weekend of retail therapy," Elizabeth said.

Sierra nodded. "I said something very similar to my husband last night. But let's take a look at the house, shall we?"

She led the way into the large reception room, which had spectacular views out to the sea.

"This would be perfect as a restaurant dining room," Elizabeth said. "People would come just for the view."

"The kitchen is through here," Sierra said.

"This is terrible," Elizabeth said when she saw the cramped and dated kitchen. "It isn't anywhere near large enough to function as a restaurant kitchen."

"There's a dining room through here," Sierra said.

Elizabeth followed her and then stood in the doorway between the rooms. "If this wall could come down, the two rooms together would just about work for a restaurant kitchen. What else is on this level?"

"A large conservatory and another reception room," Sierra told her.

After walking through both of them, Elizabeth glanced at Andy and then looked at Bessie.

"The conservatory would be lovely for small events. The other reception room is larger than I was expecting and would be similarly useful. I can imagine weddings of up to forty people could be accommodated, using both spaces."

"Let me show you the first floor," Sierra suggested.

They walked through several bedrooms and bathrooms. The second floor had even more bedrooms.

"There's plenty of room on the first floor to create a small kitchen and reception room for, um, for the owner," Elizabeth said as they began to walk back down the stairs. "That would leave the entire ground floor for the restaurant and event centre."

"So what do you think?" Sierra asked as they walked back into the large foyer.

"I think it could work as a restaurant and a home," Elizabeth said.

"Do you think people would be willing to drive all the way out here to eat?" Andy asked.

Elizabeth glanced at him and then quickly looked away. "If the restaurant was run by a particularly talented chef, then they probably would. This isn't far from where Dan and Carol used to have their restaurant, and they were always busy."

Andy sighed. "It's just such a huge decision."

"It is," Elizabeth agreed. "You shouldn't rush into anything. It's nearly as important as deciding to get married, and no one would do that in a hurry." She looked at Andy and then put a hand to her mouth. "Oops, sorry. Some people seem to be able to make that decision quite quickly."

Andy flushed. "I suppose I deserved that."

Elizabeth shrugged and then turned and walked to the window. "The views are spectacular," she said.

"They are," Andy agreed, his eyes firmly pinned on Elizabeth.

"Well," Sierra finally said, interrupting the awkward silence. "Can I answer any questions for you?"

"Has there been much interest in the property?" Bessie asked.

Sierra nodded. "I've shown it several times over the past month. If I were Mr. Caine, I would put an offer in as quickly as possible."

Andy frowned. "Is anyone else thinking of turning the property into a restaurant?"

"No one has mentioned that when I've shown them the property, but, obviously, I've no idea what people might be considering and simply not discussing with me."

"Do you think it would be difficult to get planning permission to put the restaurant here?" Bessie asked.

"Duncan assures me that it shouldn't be a problem. We can make the sale contingent on it as well," Andy told her.

"What's the asking price?" Elizabeth asked.

Sierra told her.

Elizabeth walked into the centre of the room and rotated slowly. "It would make a wonderful special event centre," she said thoughtfully. "I'd need a small kitchen, but we would only have a limited menu, so it wouldn't have to be a terribly large kitchen. This foyer would be a lovely space for weddings, actually. We could put a small platform right here and have seating all the way around the happy couple."

"You're going to buy this house out from under me," Andy said angrily.

"I didn't say that," Elizabeth replied.

"But you're thinking about it."

"You aren't the only one trying to build a small business," Elizabeth told him. "The island needs another wedding and event venue, and this place is just about perfect. I could even add a small spa and turn some of the bedrooms into treatment rooms. Maybe we could have retreat weekends and use the other bedrooms as guest rooms."

"I know you're angry with me, but I didn't expect you to try to destroy my business."

Elizabeth stared at him for a moment and then looked away "You don't have a business, not yet. I've every right to consider the location for my business. I have a number of customers for whom I'm trying to find the perfect wedding venue. Maybe I could create that for them."

"If you outbid me on this property, I'll never forgive you," Andy told her.

Elizabeth shrugged. "I have to do what's best for me. You weren't thinking of me when you got engaged to another woman. I've no reason to think of you now."

"I asked you here to help me, not so that you could buy the house out from under me."

"Perhaps you should have considered all of the possibilities before you asked me to come. You ought to have realised that I no longer have any reason to want to help you."

"I think that's quite enough," Bessie said.

Andy nodded. "It's definitely quite enough," he snapped. "Let's go," he said to Sierra.

"Did you want to go around the house again?" Sierra asked Elizabeth.

Andy sighed. "That's how it is, is it? You're going to do everything you can to help her."

"I'm going to do everything I can to sell this house," Sierra replied. "It isn't personal."

Andy looked at Elizabeth and then at Sierra. "Oh, it's personal. It's very personal."

CHAPTER 11

Elizabeth stared at Andy for a moment and then turned and walked out of the house.

Bessie gave Andy a quick hug.

"Please try to talk to her," he whispered in her ear. "I really don't want to fight her to get this house."

"It sounds as if you've made a decision, anyway," Bessie replied.

Andy chuckled. "Yeah, I have. I didn't realise how much I wanted the house until she said she wanted it." He glanced over at Sierra. "Please talk to her."

"I will," Bessie promised.

Andy sighed. "She's right, though. This would be an awesome event centre or spa or some combination of the two. If Elizabeth really wants it, she can have it."

Bessie shook her head. "Should I talk to her or not?"

"Yes, find out what she really wants. I don't want to get into a bidding war over the house. Not because of the money, but because I don't want to do anything to hurt her again. The house is hers if she wants it. I'm really hoping she doesn't, though."

"I'll ring you later today or tomorrow," Bessie promised.

"We could put an offer in now," Sierra offered. "I could ring the seller and see if we can come to an agreement immediately. Of course, I'd have to recommend that you put in a very competitive offer."

Andy nodded. "Of course you would."

"I'm just doing my job," Sierra told him.

"I'd better go. I hope Elizabeth didn't leave without me," Bessie said.

"If she did, we'll take you home," Andy promised.

Bessie gave him another hug and then rushed after Elizabeth. The young woman hadn't gone far. She was sitting in her car, staring at the sea.

"Sorry," Bessie said as she climbed into the passenger seat.

"Has he made an offer?" she asked.

"Not yet. He said that if you really want the house, he'll walk away. Otherwise, he's going to buy it, though."

Elizabeth gave her a satisfied smile. "I knew he'd never actually do anything if he wasn't pushed in some way," she said as she started the engine.

"You don't want the house?"

"I love it, and it would be perfect for what I want to do, but it's better for Andy. He needs to get his restaurant up and running. Besides, Daddy and I have been talking about turning the Douglas house into an event centre."

"It's certainly large enough."

"It's huge and no one wants to buy it. We'd have to rip out a lot of walls and make a huge number of changes, but Daddy is willing to fund the project. I think he's bored, actually, now that my brothers are running most of his businesses for him."

Bessie nodded. "It will take a long time to get the house ready."

"I'll bet we'll have it done before Andy finishes his restaurant," Elizabeth replied. "In fact, I think I'll tell him that. He'll see it as a challenge."

"You're doing your best to help him."

"I am, even though he doesn't deserve my help."

Bessie patted her arm. "He's a good person."

"I know, and I still care deeply about him. I hope my threatening to buy the house pushes him to make an offer. Once he's bought the place, then I'll make sure he knows that Daddy and I are working on the Douglas house. That should be all he needs to hear to start working on his restaurant."

"Douglas is a better location for an event centre."

"It is, and we already own the house, so we can start working on it whenever we want. I might take Daddy's designer through next week and see what she thinks."

"That will give you an advantage over Andy."

"I have all sorts of advantages over Andy," Elizabeth said with a laugh.

Bessie laughed with her. "What shall I tell him when I ring him?"

"Tell him that I'm prepared to let him have the house because I think the Douglas house is in a better location for what I want. It's also larger, with more bedrooms and reception spaces, so I truly can have spa weekends and things there. Andy's new house is a bit too small, really, but don't tell him I said that."

"I hope he doesn't start worrying that he should be in Douglas, too."

"He won't. We all know that people will drive from all over the island to eat at Andy's restaurant once it's open. Being out in Lonan will mean he'll have plenty of parking. That's an advantage over most of Douglas."

"Your house has lots of parking."

Elizabeth nodded. "But there aren't all that many houses in Douglas as large as ours."

"I don't think there are any other houses in Douglas that are that size."

"You may be right. But that's enough about all of that. What shall we do for lunch?"

"We're having lunch?"

"Of course we're having lunch. I have to do something to thank you for giving up your morning for me."

"I was happy to do it. I want you and Andy to be happy."

Elizabeth sighed. "If you don't mind, I'd much prefer it if you didn't put our names together in that way."

"I'm sorry. I didn't mean to upset you."

"I'm not upset, just sad. He looked really nice today, didn't he? I don't think I'd ever seen that shirt before."

"He's a very attractive young man."

"Jennifer might have gone after him even if he weren't rich."

"Perhaps. I'm certain there are several other young women on the island who are hoping to catch his eye."

Elizabeth frowned. "What about the pub in Laxey? I haven't been there in ages. When I first moved to the island, I used to have my friends from across visit, and we used to spend a lot of time in that pub."

"That's fine with me. The food is good there."

Elizabeth had been driving aimlessly around the island, following a twisty road that Bessie wasn't certain she'd ever seen before. Now she made a sharp right turn, and within a minute Bessie knew exactly where they were. They parked at the pub a few minutes later.

"Shepherd's pie," Bessie said after she'd looked at the menu.

"Oh, that does sound good. We have a new chef, and he seems to think that he has to make fancy food all the time. He makes Mum whatever she wants, of course, but Daddy and I get chicken and leeks in wine sauce or beef Wellington every night."

Bessie stared at her for a moment. "And you're complaining?" she asked eventually.

Elizabeth flushed. "I'm sorry. I know I sounded unbelievably spoiled. I know I have been unbelievably spoiled, actually. I just meant that something simple and comforting such as shepherd's pie sounds truly wonderful, that's all."

Bessie nodded and then waited while Elizabeth went to the bar to place their order.

"If you were me, would you forgive Andy?" Elizabeth asked as she slid back into her seat.

"I'm not going to answer that. I'm not you, and I can't even begin to understand how you feel. What I will say is that if you do forgive him, you need to forgive him completely and promise yourself, if not him, that you'll never mention it again. You can't tell him he's forgiven and then bring the subject up every time you have a disagreement."

Elizabeth sighed. "I am rather prone to doing that."

"Most people are, to the detriment of their relationships."

"How did you get so wise?"

Bessie flushed. "I've always enjoyed talking to people and hearing about their lives. And unlike most people, I listen."

Elizabeth laughed. While they enjoyed their meal and then pudding, the pair talked about the weather, Elizabeth's childhood in England, and Bessie's experiences growing up in the US.

"That was delicious, but I'm very full," Bessie said as she pushed her empty pudding plate towards the centre of the table.

"It was good. I suppose I can afford the extra calories. I've lost quite a lot of weight now that Andy isn't cooking for me any longer."

"I suspect worry about your mother has been keeping you from eating as well."

"Yes, of course. I truly mustn't blame Andy for everything. Although to be fair, I'm quite happy that I've lost a bit of weight. My clothes were starting to get a bit snug before our holiday."

"Don't most people gain weight on holiday?"

"Perhaps I would have gained if I hadn't spent most of the holiday in various hospitals and treatment centres."

Bessie frowned. "I hope your mother is feeling better."

"Ah, I nearly forgot. She wanted me to invite you to tea one day next week. If you're too busy with the cold case unit to do it next week, she doesn't mind waiting until the following week."

"Let me check my calendar when we get back to my cottage. If I can't manage next week, I believe the following week is completely free."

Elizabeth drove them back to Bessie's and then waited while Bessie checked her calendar and gave her a date. "I'll ring you if that won't work for Mum. She does have rather a lot of appointments these days, but she tries to get them all out of the way first thing in the morning."

"Let me know if you need to change anything. Otherwise, I'll be at Thie yn Traie around two."

Elizabeth nodded. "Thank you again for coming with me this morning. Tell Andy I'll let him have it, but tell him he needs to hurry or I might change my mind."

Bessie laughed. "I will."

She let the young woman out and then rushed up to her bedroom to get ready for the cold case unit meeting. After changing clothes, she combed her hair and powdered her nose. It took her only a moment to unlock her desk and grab her case file. She was standing in her kitchen when Andrew arrived.

"How was your morning?" she asked as he turned the car towards Ramsey.

"It was good. Matt and I had a nice brisk walk at the Point of Ayre. We took pictures of the lighthouse, and then we had a decent lunch in Bride."

"The café is still there?"

"No, it's not, but there's a little pub near where you said the café used to be."

Bessie frowned. "A pub? Has someone reopened the Cow and Cart?"

"It wasn't called the Cow and Cart, but I'm fairly certain it used to be."

"Oh?"

Andrew laughed. "It's now called the Mouse and Walrus, but the interior decorations don't reflect that. I'd say they reflect the old name. For instance, the signs on the loos were in the shape of a cow and a bull, and the tables were designed to look as if they'd been made from parts of old wooden carts."

"So they didn't bother to redecorate the interior. Whoever bought it simply changed the name."

"It certainly seems that way."

"Perhaps the new owners will redecorate eventually."

"Perhaps."

They rode in silence for a short while before Andrew made a noise. "I almost forgot. Okay, I did forget. John found out some things about the owner of the car that we followed last night and the house where it was parked."

"What did he discover?"

"The car's owner is a man named Francis Farmer."

Bessie frowned. "I don't believe I've ever heard the name before."

"Unfortunately, it was more familiar to John."

"Oh dear."

"Francis moved to the island about a year ago. He works for one of the banks, although his job may well be in jeopardy if he doesn't get his drinking under control."

"What a shame."

"He's been involved in two different pub brawls in the past year. The first time there were several witnesses who all insisted that the other guy swung first. The second time the witnesses couldn't agree on what had happened."

Bessie sighed. "And now he's seeing Delores."

"It certainly seems that way. John rang a few people, and one of them told him that Francis hasn't been out drinking nearly as much since he got his new girlfriend."

"I suppose that's a good thing."

"Apparently he's also been bragging about being in line for a large inheritance soon, too."

Bessie frowned. "He's going to kill Hazel."

"We've no evidence of that, but John has rung Pete, and the Douglas Constabulary is going to keep a close eye on Hazel's house. They're hoping to catch her going in or out, but of course they can't watch the house all day long."

"Maybe we should."

"Are you serious?"

Bessie shrugged. "I don't know what to do. I'm worried about Hazel." She shook her head. "What else did John learn?"

"The house where Francis is living is owned by a Douglas investment company. John's going to see if he can find out whose names are on the lease agreement."

"And we still aren't any closer to finding Hazel."

"On the contrary. I think we're a good deal closer to finding Hazel. We have to assume that she's still living in her home in Douglas, even if she wasn't there when we visited. And we know that Delores and Francis visit her, at least occasionally."

"What if they've already killed her and they were just there – I don't know, tidying up the mess?"

"It's a possibility, but there are dozens of possibilities. Pete and his men and women will be watching Hazel's house. John is going to have his team keep an eye on Francis and Delores. I suggest we try visiting again tomorrow morning. Hopefully Francis will be at work."

Bessie nodded. "And now we need to turn our attention to our cold case. I hope you have some new information to share, because I feel as if we're at a dead end right now."

"It's definitely a frustrating case, but I do have some new information. I'm not certain it's going to help in any way, but we can hope."

He pulled his car into the Seaview's car park and found a space near the entrance. Bessie sighed as they crossed to the building's front door.

"I ate too much lunch," she said. "And I had pudding. Jasper has promised us something special today, and I think I'm too full to enjoy it."

"I'm certain you'll be able to find room for a little something."

Bessie laughed. "I suspect you're right."

Jasper was standing in the lobby, frowning at the couches.

"Good afternoon," Bessie greeted him.

"Is it?" he demanded. "These couches need to be at least four inches more to the left."

"Do you want us to help you move them?" Andrew asked.

Jasper shook his head. "I have a crew on the way. They're going to move the couches until I think they're in the perfect spot."

"Or maybe you could simply go into your office and take a few deep breaths," Bessie suggested.

Jasper frowned. "If anyone else in the world said that to me, I'd be very angry."

"But you can't be angry at me because you know I have your best interests at heart."

"Yes, of course, but everyone is being impossible right now."

"All the more reason for you to be kind to your staff."

"I am kind to my staff."

"Making them move couches by inches is not kind."

Jasper sighed. "You're right, of course. I think I simply wanted to do something that I could control. I certainly can't control the chef, or the pastry chef, or the assistant sous-chef, who isn't even meant to have that title."

"Oh?"

"It doesn't matter. It's a very long story, and I'd really rather I didn't have to think about it."

"Where is our meeting today?" Andrew asked.

"You're in the penthouse again. I thought it would be nice for you, especially since I've rather let you down again in the catering department."

"We're only paying for coffee, tea, and biscuits," Bessie reminded him.

"But I promised you something nicer today, and I'm not certain I delivered. As my chefs can't get along long enough to do anything productive, I went to that new bakery near the shops and bought you some fairy cakes. I had my staff put them on fancy trays, but, honestly, they don't look very tasty. Just in case, I had them give you a tray of biscuits, too, but they're just shop-bought."

"It doesn't matter," Bessie said firmly. "You worry about your chef and your pastry chef and your couches, if you must. We'll be just fine."

Jasper grinned at her. "You may be fine, but I do feel as if young Hugh will be quite disappointed."

Bessie laughed. "Hugh will be fine, too. He's old enough to handle a bit of disappointment."

"I'm sorry to interrupt," a young man said as he approached them. "Chef wanted me to tell you that he's not making any puddings tonight," he told Jasper.

"Tell Chef that…" Jasper trailed off and then sighed. "I'd better go and deal with this," he told Bessie and Andrew. "Let me know what you think of the fairy cakes. I may be buying all of our puddings from that bakery from now on."

Bessie and Andrew watched as Jasper and the other man walked away, heading towards the restaurant.

"Shall we?" Andrew asked as they disappeared from view.

The lift carried them to the top floor. Andrew pushed open the conference room door. Bessie walked in and stopped.

"Jasper was correct. I'm not certain I want to try those fairy cakes."

Andrew raised an eyebrow as he looked at the table at the back of the room. "The colours are, um, unnatural."

"The rainbows would be pretty if we weren't expected to eat them. I think I'll try a chocolate one," Bessie said, feeling as if she was being incredibly brave. "I never thought plain brown icing could look so tempting."

Andrew filled a plate with biscuits while Bessie carried her fairy cake and a cup of tea to her place. A few minutes later, everyone else had arrived. Harry hadn't wanted anything. Charles took a few biscuits, one fairy cake, and a cup of coffee. John and Doona had each taken a chocolate fairy cake along with a few biscuits.

Behind a plate full of fairy cakes decorated in lurid colours, Hugh beamed. "I hope we have some new information," he said before he bit into his first cake.

CHAPTER 12

Andrew nodded. "I have updated information on the handful of people who were considered witnesses. Sherry has also done her best to try to find answers to our questions."

"So where is everyone now?" Charles asked as Andrew took a sip of tea.

"Start with the boyfriend," Doona said. "He may be a lovely man, but I'm always suspicious of the significant others."

"He's at the top of my list," Hugh said. "Assuming that something bad happened to Michelle and Dazaray, that is."

"I wouldn't be surprised if Luke is now married with children of his own," Charles said. "It's been ten years."

"It has been ten years," Andrew agreed. "But apparently Luke is still holding out hope that Michelle will come back one day. He's still living in the same place and working the same job. He told Sherry that he doesn't want to go anywhere, as that might make it more difficult for Michelle to find him when she returns."

"Is he sweetly romantic or delusional?" Doona asked.

"Sherry noted that he became very upset when she suggested that he might want to move on with his life," Andrew replied. "Obviously, I'm going to give you all copies of the interviews so you can draw your own conclusions from what Luke had to say."

"Did Sherry ask him for more information about Michelle and Dazaray?" Bessie asked. "I'm thinking about the things we discussed, such as how trusting Michelle might have been, or whether Dazaray might have run off."

"She did, and Luke told her that Michelle was almost too trusting. He said that he could see her getting into a car with a stranger if the stranger told a convincing enough story," Andrew replied.

Bessie frowned. "Even if she had Dazaray with her?"

"According to Luke, yes. He also said that Dazaray was inclined to run off, which is why Michelle had put her in the pushchair that evening. Apparently, that was the only way Michelle could get her home safely."

"Except they never got home," Bessie said sadly.

"They may have," Andrew replied. "Remember that we asked Sherry to consider whether Michelle and Dazaray spent some time at home after their dinner with Luke. Sherry has gone back through all of the reports, and she talked to Michelle's parents at length about the idea. The conclusion she reached is that it's possible Michelle and Dazaray came home, but there's no evidence to support the idea."

"It would be more accurate to say that there isn't any evidence to confirm or refute the idea," Charles suggested. "Both options seem equally likely, really."

Andrew made a note. "That's a good point, actually."

"What about Michelle's parents?" Doona asked. "Where are they now?"

"They, too, are still living in the same place," Andrew told them. "They're both still working, although her father is considering retiring soon. Sherry told me that they both appear to have aged a great deal more than ten years, which she assumed was due primarily to worry about their daughter and granddaughter."

"Did she say the same about Luke?" Bessie asked.

Andrew checked his notes. "Not in those exact words, anyway."

"I believe, when people go missing, it is usually hardest on the missing person's parents over anyone else," Charles said. "I would have been suspicious of Michelle's parents if Sherry hadn't made that sort of comment. I wouldn't expect anyone else involved in the case to be as affected."

"What did they have to say about the likelihood of Michelle trusting a stranger?" Hugh asked.

"Interestingly, they didn't agree with Luke," Andrew replied. "Of course, they aren't aware of what Luke said in his interview, but they both agreed that Michelle was wary of strangers, especially when she had Dazaray with her."

"That makes Luke appear even more guilty," Doona said.

"Were Stanley and Jessica interviewed together or separately?" Bessie asked.

"They were interviewed separately," Andrew told her. "They gave nearly identical answers to that question and to the question of whether Dazaray might have run off. According to them, Dazaray was very well behaved and never ran away. They also both insisted that Michelle would have kept her in the pushchair until they were inside the house because she worried about Dazaray after dark."

"Interesting," Bessie said, making a note.

"What did they have to say about Michelle's relationship with Luke?" Doona asked.

Andrew smiled. "That's where they didn't agree, at least not completely. Stanley had nothing but good things to say about Luke, but Jessica was a bit more circumspect with her comments."

"What did she say?" Bessie looked up from her notebook.

"It wasn't so much what she said as how she said it," Andrew explained. "Sherry took notes and highlighted some of Jessica's answers when she sent me the updated interviews."

"Meaning what?" John asked.

Andrew flipped through his notes. "You can read it all for yourselves later, but one answer that Sherry highlighted had to do with whether Michelle and Luke ever argued. Apparently, Stanley simply waved a hand and said something about how all couples argue but that the pair were devoted to one another. Jessica, on the other hand, said that she was unaware of any recent argument between the pair."

"Unaware and recent," John said. "Those are both troubling words in that context."

Andrew nodded. "As I said, you can read more in the reports."

"Are they still in contact with Luke?" Doona wondered.

"They are. Apparently, he often celebrates holidays with them. Besides Christmas and Easter, they have small family gatherings for birthdays, including Michelle's and Dazaray's."

Bessie frowned. "He joins them to celebrate Michelle's birthday each year?"

"So I'm told."

"Was Luke asked about Michelle's relationship with her parents?" Hugh asked.

"He was, and he told Sherry that Michelle sometimes complained about having to live at home with her parents and her daughter, but that she was truly grateful to them for being there when Dylan passed away. He said that he and Michelle were both looking forward to getting their own place soon so that Michelle could move out."

"Why couldn't she simply move in with him?" Bessie asked.

"He said they wanted a clean start living somewhere where neither of them had lived before."

"I suppose that makes some sense," Doona said, sounding doubtful.

Andrew glanced at the clock. "I want to give you plenty of time to read through the interviews before we meet again tomorrow. We've only two more people to discuss."

"Michelle's two closest friends," Charles said "April and Krista."

Andrew nodded. "Let's start with April, because everyone identified her as Michelle's closest friend."

"So where is she now?" Doona asked.

Andrew swallowed a bite of fairy cake and made a face. "They aren't great, are they?" he asked.

"I thought they were good," Hugh protested. "My standards aren't all that high, though."

Everyone laughed while Andrew consulted his notes.

"April is still living in Dover. By her own admission, she's become something of a recluse since Michelle disappeared. The incident has made her considerably more wary of strangers."

"How sad," Bessie said.

"She's still working the same job, and she told Sherry that she often feels as if her life is on hold until she finds out what happened to Michelle."

"What a shame," Doona said. "It seems increasingly likely that we're not going to be able to solve this one. No one may ever know what happened to Michelle."

"What did she say about Michelle's relationship with Luke and with her parents?" John asked.

"She said that, as far as she knew, Luke and Michelle were deeply in love. She felt he was a much better choice than Dylan had been, and that Michelle was lucky to have him."

"Interesting," Doona said.

"She also said that Michelle and her parents had been getting along quite well, considering the circumstances," Andrew added. "Apparently, they hadn't cared for Dylan, but they'd been very supportive of Michelle since she'd moved back to Dover, and they'd done everything they could to help her with Dazaray."

"What about Michelle trusting strangers or Dazaray running off?" John asked.

"April seemed to think that Michelle would have been cautious if anyone had approached her, but she also said that Michelle was quick to consider people friends, even if they'd met only once or twice in passing."

"So anyone could have seen her in a shop and said hello a few times and then convinced her to get in a car," Charles said.

"April seemed to think so, anyway. She also said that Dazaray was usually very good, but that she'd seen the little girl run away from Michelle occasionally. She agreed with Luke, that Michelle would have kept Dazaray in the pushchair until they'd reached home."

"That just leaves Krista," Bessie said. "Before we talk about her, what does April think of Krista? We did ask Sherry to ask everyone questions about everyone else, didn't we? We haven't been talking about the friends, though."

"Luke had nice things to say about April, but stated that he barely knew Krista. Apparently, April and Michelle spent a lot of time together, but Michelle spent time with Krista only to allow their children to play together."

"You did say that Krista had a child around the same age as Dazaray."

Andrew nodded. "Stanley said he liked April well enough

and that he'd only met Krista once or twice. Jessica told Sherry that she considered April almost another daughter, as she and Michelle had been friends for nearly all of their lives. She said she'd met Krista a handful of times and that she seemed nice enough."

"And what did April have to say about Krista?" Bessie wondered.

"She said that Krista was Michelle's mum friend and that the only reason that they were friends was because they had children the same age. From what I read, I got the impression that April wasn't terribly fond of Krista."

"And what did Krista have to say about April?" John asked.

"We'll get to that," Andrew replied. "Let's start with where Krista is now and then we'll work through what she had to say about everyone."

There's something there, Bessie thought. *Otherwise, Andrew would have simply answered the question.*

"So where is Krista now?" John asked.

"She's still in the same place. She had another child about a year after Michelle disappeared. When her second child was two, she went back to work at the shop where she'd worked with Michelle."

"And what did she have to say about everyone?" Bessie asked.

"Krista told Sherry that she didn't think that Michelle was very close to her parents. As she put it, Michelle left home at eighteen, which says something about her relationship with her mother and father."

"That isn't what she said the first time she was questioned," Hugh said.

"I went back and reread both of Krista's earlier interviews," Andrew replied. "Her answers back then were considerably more vague."

"Did she say anything else about Michelle's parents?" Bessie asked.

"She told Sherry that they'd never cared for Dylan, which upset Michelle. She also said that they were very fond of Luke and that Michelle felt as if she had to stay with him just to keep them happy."

"Does that mean that she wasn't really happy with Luke?" Doona asked.

"According to Krista, they were having some problems. When Sherry tried to push her for more information, she said something along the lines of 'everyone complains to friends about their boyfriends,' and refused to say anything else."

Bessie frowned. "There's more to it than that," she said.

Andrew nodded. "I thought so, too. When asked what she thought of Luke, Krista said that she'd met him only once or twice and couldn't possibly comment."

"Sherry needs to talk to her again," John said. "She knows something, or she suspects something, at least."

"What did she have to say about April?" Doona wondered.

"She said that Michelle had very little in common with April now that she had Dazaray. Apparently, Michelle sometimes complained that April always expected her to drop everything whenever she wanted to do something, and didn't appreciate that Michelle always put Dazaray first."

"I feel as if Krista knew her far better than anyone else thought she did," Bessie said. "And far better than she let on when she was questioned initially."

Andrew nodded. "You can read her statement for yourself, but I got the same impression. The interview started out much the same as her previous ones, but once Sherry started asking her very specific questions about the other people in Michelle's life, Krista told her a good deal more."

"From the sound of it, Michelle was closer to Krista

than anyone else in the months before she disappeared," Charles said. "I think Sherry needs to talk to her again. It may well be that Krista knows exactly what happened to Michelle."

"Sherry and I discussed that. The problem is, Krista has kept quiet for ten years now. We have to find a way to convince her to share what she knows," Andrew said.

"If Michelle did leave voluntarily, she must have been running away from someone or something," Bessie said thoughtfully. "Krista must believe that she's helping to protect her friend by keeping quiet."

"We need to know more about Michelle's relationship with Luke," Doona said. "Maybe he was abusing her, or maybe he did something to Dazaray."

"I think Krista knows a lot more than she's let on over the years," Bessie said. "Sherry needs to persuade her to talk. Maybe Sherry can convince her to ask Michelle to get in touch. No one else has to know that Sherry has spoken to her, do they?"

"Sherry would want to close the case, but there may be a way for her to do so without anyone finding out," Andrew replied.

"There are ways," Charles said. "If Sherry has any questions, have her ring me. Over the years, I've been involved in a number of cases where we've not let anyone know when we've found a missing person."

"What about any of the other possibilities?" Harry asked. "It's still possible that Michelle and her daughter were taken off the street by a known predator or someone involved in human trafficking."

"Sherry has done her best to investigate that side of things," Andrew said. "So far she hasn't found anything suspicious, but she hasn't yet exhausted all of the possibilities."

"She thinks Michelle left voluntarily and Krista helped her," Harry said.

Andrew nodded. "That's the conclusion she came to after this last round of interviews."

"I'm not certain I agree, but I'll reserve judgement until after I've read the interviews," Harry said.

"What about the possibility that Luke killed them and disposed of the bodies somewhere?" Hugh asked.

"Sherry thinks that, if that was what had happened, Luke would have moved elsewhere by now. She also thinks that the bodies would have turned up at some time over the past ten years."

"She's probably right about the second part, anyway. Bodies don't tend to go unnoticed – not for ten years," Harry said. "Not unless Luke, or someone else, found an especially clever hiding place."

"If it was Luke who killed them, he had twenty-four hours to get rid of the bodies," John said. "That's a very long time."

"But he didn't have a car, did he?" Bessie asked. "I thought I read that in his initial interview."

"He didn't have a car when Michelle disappeared," Andrew confirmed. "He told the inspector doing the initial investigation that he felt responsible for Michelle's disappearance because he should have driven her and Dazaray home after dinner, but he'd been in a car accident a month earlier and his car had been a total write-off. As he could walk to work and back, he hadn't yet bothered to find a replacement."

"And he allowed the police to go through his flat when they came to question him about the disappearances," Doona said. "I don't know that he would have been able to get rid of the bodies and clean up the flat that quickly."

Bessie shuddered. "I'm really hoping that Krista is the key

to all of this. She knows more than she's admitted to this point. Sherry needs to find out everything that she knows."

Andrew nodded. "I think you're right. I'm going to suggest to Sherry that she pursue that line of investigation for now and leave the others until either the case is solved or she's certain that she's learned all she can from Krista."

"We could all go down to Dover and question her ourselves," Doona suggested. "That would be far less frustrating than sitting here waiting to hear back from Sherry."

"You know we can't do that," Andrew said. "Sherry is going to go back and talk to Krista again tomorrow morning, though, so we might not have to wait too long to hear more."

"She's been keeping secrets for a long time. She's not going to want to give them up," Bessie said.

"Sherry and I talked about different things she might say to her to try to persuade her to talk. If any of you have any ideas, I'd love to hear them," Andrew said.

"Presumably, if Michelle didn't get along well with her parents, then trying to convince her that Dazaray's grandparents deserve to be a part of her life won't work," Doona said.

"Sherry said that Krista told her that Stanley and Jessica had both made comments on how Dazaray was half Dylan and that they couldn't wait for another grandchild with a – quote – proper father," Andrew said.

"How horrible of them," Bessie exclaimed. "I do hope Dazaray didn't hear their nasty remarks."

"And if Michelle was running away from Luke, the fact that he's still waiting for her to come back probably won't make Krista want to tell anyone where she is," Charles said.

"It may well have the opposite effect," Doona said. "If I'd run away from a man, the last thing I'd want to hear is that he's still waiting ten years later for me to come back."

Andrew nodded. "Krista did have some nice things to say

about April. She understood how close April and Michelle had once been, even if they had grown apart since Dazaray arrived."

"Maybe Sherry should tell Krista how miserable April is because she's still missing her friend so badly," Bessie suggested. "You said April has almost become a recluse and that she worries a lot about strangers. Maybe Sherry can convince Krista to say just enough to put April's fears to rest."

Andrew made a note. "I'll suggest that, but I don't know if it will work. We could be wrong about Krista, too. She may not know anything more than what she's already told Sherry."

"What did Krista say about how trusting Michelle was or about the likelihood of Dazaray running off?" Bessie asked as people began to put away their things.

"She said that life had taught Michelle not to trust anyone and that Michelle had trained Dazaray to stay close to her and not speak to strangers," Andrew replied.

"Interesting," Bessie said. "Although it's difficult to know whom to believe."

"I believe Krista," Doona said. "And I think she knows exactly where Michelle is right now."

"I hope you're right," Andrew told her. "There's nothing I'd like better than a happy ending."

The group chatted for a few additional minutes, and Andrew gave them their copies of the most recent interviews before people finished gathering their things and began to head for the door.

"Feel free to take a few fairy cakes back to your cottages with you," Andrew said to Harry and Charles as they crossed the room.

"Thanks, but I don't eat such things," Harry said.

Charles made a face. "I do, but the one I had wasn't particularly good. I'll pass, thanks."

As the two men left the room, Doona sighed. "I hate to say it, but Charles was right. The fairy cake that I had was not very good."

"I thought they were okay," Hugh said. "I'll take what's left home to Grace and Aalish."

He packed the remaining cakes back into one of the bakery's boxes that had been left under the table. As he did that, John and Doona hugged Bessie and then left the room.

"Ready to go?" Andrew asked Bessie as Hugh finished gathering his things.

Bessie nodded and then picked up her handbag and the envelope with the case file. She glanced at the table in the back of the room and then shook her head. "We should go somewhere that does nice cakes for dinner tonight," she said. "I'd like to forget all about the one I had here today."

CHAPTER 13

"What would you like to do now?" Andrew asked as they got into his car.

Bessie thought for a moment. "I think I need a walk on the beach," she said. "I'm worried about Hazel, and I need to read the reports on the recent interviews, but mostly I need to clear my head. We can go back to Laxey or walk on the beach here, whichever you'd prefer."

"Let's go back to Laxey," Andrew said. "I want to ring Sherry with all of our comments from today."

Bessie nodded and then settled back and watched the scenery go past as Andrew drove them back to her cottage. Once there, she put her case file inside Treoghe Bwaane and immediately headed out for her walk.

"I may follow you shortly, or I may end up talking to Sherry for hours," Andrew said as she walked past him as he was opening the door to his cottage.

"I may walk up and down several times. I have a lot on my mind."

Andrew nodded and then went inside. Bessie walked down to the water's edge and then began a slow stroll along the wet sand. Inhaling deeply, she tried to get her thoughts to stop spinning.

"Bessie, hello," a voice said a moment later.

Bessie stopped and looked up at the row of holiday cottages. Charles was waving from behind the one where he was staying on this visit.

"Hello," she replied.

"Do you mind if I walk with you for a short while?" he asked.

"Of course not," she replied automatically.

Charles chuckled. "You'd say that regardless, wouldn't you?"

"Probably, but you are more than welcome."

They walked in silence for a minute before Charles spoke again.

"Do you often think about Matthew?" he asked.

Bessie gasped. It wasn't a question she'd been expecting. While she tried to work out how to reply, Charles held up a hand.

"I'm sorry. That was a rude question. Is the weather always this lovely in August?"

"Actually, it often rains in the summer. It's been very dry this week, though. And, yes, I do think of Matthew often. I think of him every day when I get dressed because I use a dusting powder that reminds me of him."

He sighed. "Does it ever get any easier? Sometimes I feel as if I might, ah, but never mind."

"You lost someone you loved," Bessie said, trying to remember what she'd heard about the man's past.

"I lost the only woman I've ever loved. Mandy was so beautiful. I thought we were going to be together forever."

"I won't ask what happened, because I don't want to pry, but if you want to talk about it, I'm happy to listen."

"That was very well done. I don't want to talk about it. I

never want to talk about it. But I suppose I should talk about it. Maybe, if I do, I'll find peace in some way."

"Time hasn't helped?"

"I suppose it has helped to some degree," he replied. "It's made the pain less sharp, but more poignant. I always thought that I'd get married and have children, but I've never done either. I never actually imagined growing old alone, but here we are."

"I'm sorry."

He shrugged. "I suppose my mistake was falling in love when I was only sixteen. If things had gone differently, we probably would have had a stupid fight and ended things before I turned seventeen. Instead, I feel forever trapped, waiting for things to either end properly or, I don't know, pick back up where they left off, I suppose."

"She disappeared?"

"She did. The day after her sixteenth birthday. I still can't quite wrap my head around it. One day we were madly in love and planning for our future together, and the next day she was simply gone."

"I assume the police were involved."

"I don't know. Isn't that awful? I simply don't know." He stopped and stared out at the sea for a full minute. Bessie waited next to him until he spoke again.

"I can't talk about it, not right now. Maybe one day."

Before Bessie could reply, he turned and walked back down the beach towards his cottage. For a moment, Bessie was tempted to go after him, but she knew better than to pry. She watched him let himself into his cottage and then turned around and continued on her way.

She walked until she was halfway between Thie yn Traie and the row of new houses and then turned around. The walk back seemed to go much more quickly, but at least she felt as if her head was clearing. As she passed the last of the holiday cottages, she heard someone loudly calling her name.

"Bessie? Bessie?"

Forcing herself to smile, Bessie turned and walked up the beach towards the last cottage. She had been wondering if Maggie was avoiding her. It had been a while since she'd seen the woman. Now Bessie was curious whether Maggie would say anything about how, just a few months earlier, she'd been convinced that Dan Ross was trying to kill her.

"Good afternoon, Maggie," Bessie said.

"Is it?" Maggie asked. "You know I never complain, but we've had three cancellations in the past two days, and for the first time ever, we've no waiting list of people hoping we might be able to accommodate them. I'd blame the company in Douglas that handles our bookings, but we stopped using them months ago and it hasn't made any difference."

"I am sorry."

Maggie shrugged. "It doesn't help that Pat is away at his sister's wedding. He's been invaluable to us, managing things from down here, but now he's away and Thomas and I are having to drive down here at all hours of the day and night."

Pat was a young man who'd been homeless when Bessie had first encountered him. He'd been breaking into the last cottage in the row and sleeping on the floor there in order to escape the worst of the island's weather. Bessie had introduced him to Thomas and Maggie, and they'd been willing to put him to work and give him a chance to turn his life around. So far, both parties had seemed to be benefitting from the arrangement.

"He'll be back soon, won't he?"

"If he comes back. I'm not certain he will. He was very eager to see his sister and it wouldn't surprise me if he simply decided to stay with her and not return."

"Have you heard from him since he's been gone?"

"Oh, yes, he rings me nearly every day," Maggie told her. "He told me all about the wedding and all about his sister and her new husband. They've been taking good care of him and making him realise how important family can be."

"How lovely for him."

"Yes, of course, but what about me?" Maggie wailed. "I can't take care of the cottages by myself, and Thomas still isn't able to do much of anything. He's better, now that the weather is improved, but he's still weak and he tires very easily. I'm not certain he'll ever get back to his old self."

"I'm sorry to hear that. I'm very fond of Thomas."

"He'll be fine," Maggie said, blinking back tears. "But how are you? How is the latest cold case? Are you going to solve it?"

"I'm fine. The latest cold case is challenging. I've no idea if we'll solve it or not."

Maggie nodded and then took a step closer to Bessie. "You will, though, won't you? You'll have the killer behind bars in no time at all, won't you?"

"We don't always look at murder investigations. Sometimes we consider other sorts of crimes, like missing persons."

"Most missing people were probably murdered. You need to look at the husband or the wife. He or she probably buried the body under the patio or something."

Bessie stared at her for a moment and then shrugged. "I'll keep that in mind."

"Anything is possible."

"I suppose so," Bessie replied. She took a step away from the woman and then stopped. "Do you know Hazel Lace?" she asked. Maggie lived for gossip, and it often seemed to Bessie as if the woman knew everyone on the island.

"Hazel Lace?" Maggie repeated. "Is that Delores's mum?"

"It is, yes."

"I don't really know her, but I know Delores."

"When was the last time you spoke to her?"

"To Delores? Last week. I haven't spoken to Hazel in years, probably, though."

"I've been trying to find Hazel," Bessie explained. "But I don't have a number for Delores, and none of my friends seem to know how to contact her."

"She moves around a lot, living with different guys. She has a history of picking losers, too. The current one is a good example."

"Oh?"

Maggie shrugged. "His name is Francis, but he wants everyone to call him Frank. I can't remember his surname, but it doesn't much matter. He and Delores won't be together for long."

"Why not?"

"Delores won't put up with him forever. She always falls for idiots, but it never takes her long to realise her mistake."

"She's been married several times."

"But after her last divorce she told everyone she's never getting married again. I can't see Frank lasting much longer, really. She'll get tired of him telling her what to do all the time, or he'll get tired of listening to her complain about everything. Either way, Delores will be looking for somewhere else to live soon."

"She's living with Frank?"

"Oh, yeah. He rents a place in Ramsey somewhere. I'm not certain exactly where it is, but it isn't far from the Swine and Swallow."

Bessie frowned. She knew that the police were often called to the Swine and Swallow to break up fights and clear up car crashes in the pub's small car park. "Is that where he drinks?"

"He picked that house especially so that he can walk to the pub. You know it isn't safe to park there."

"Interesting."

Maggie shrugged. "I don't know why it's interesting, but I do know that he and Delores will be there tonight. It's Quiz Night and Frank loves Quiz Night. He's not very bright, but his head is full of useless trivia. They often win."

"What time tonight?"

"Quiz Night starts at seven, but Frank and Delores will probably be there earlier. You aren't thinking of going to the Swine and Swallow, are you?"

"I might be. I'd quite like a word with Delores."

Maggie frowned. "Take John with you. Better yet, take John and Hugh with you. The Swine and Swallow can be rough."

"I'll probably take Andrew with me."

"No offense, I know he's a retired police inspector and all that, but he's, well, he's not the youngest of men. You'd be better off with John and Hugh, and maybe a few off-duty constables as well."

"I can't believe the pub is that bad."

"Believe what you want, just be careful."

Bessie nodded. "Thank you."

"And good luck with Delores. She can be difficult."

Bessie nodded. "I just want her to tell me how to reach Hazel. It's a fairly simple question."

Maggie laughed. "Don't be surprised if you don't get a simple answer."

As Bessie continued along the beach, she tried to think of a plan. It was already getting late, and she was hungry, but if Frank and Delores were going to be at the pub early, it was probably best to try to find them there before the pub got busy with Quiz Night. She was lost in thought when someone touched her arm.

Jumping, she swallowed a scream as she turned to look at the man next to her.

"I didn't mean to startle you," Harry said quickly.

Bessie exhaled slowly. "I was a million miles away and didn't even know you were there until you touched my arm."

"I am sorry."

"It's fine. I should be paying more attention to the world around me, really."

"You must have something quite serious on your mind. I can't imagine it's our current cold case."

"No, it's not. I'm trying to find a friend, and I've been told that her daughter might be at a particular pub tonight. I was trying to decide whether it was worth going to see her or not."

"Maybe you should tell me the whole story."

Bessie nodded and then, as they walked together down the beach, she told Harry all about Hazel.

"So your friend might be missing or she might not," Harry concluded when Bessie was finished speaking.

"I don't know what to think. The invalid number is worrying, but I'm mostly concerned that she's put her house on the market. I wouldn't have expected her to ever do that."

"And your friend has continued to go to the house at random intervals and has yet to find Hazel at home?"

"As far as I know, yes. She told me that she'd keep trying and that she'd let me know if Hazel ever answered her door."

"It seems to me that you have two options," Harry said as they approached Treoghe Bwaane. "You can try to find Delores in the pub tonight, or you can try visiting Hazel's house while you know that Delores and Frank are otherwise occupied."

"That's a brilliant idea. I should have thought of that."

"It has the advantage of keeping you away from the Swine and Swallow. I had a few drinks there one night when I was staying at the Seaview. It's by no means the worst pub I've ever been in, but it's a bit rough around the edges, let's say."

Bessie nodded, her mind still racing. "We'd need to be certain that Delores and Frank were actually at the pub," she said. "Then we could go into Douglas and see if Hazel is at home."

"I'd be happy to go and spend a few hours in the Swine and Swallow. I'll make Charles go with me," Harry offered. "We can watch for Delores and Frank and then keep an eye on them if they turn up. You and Andrew can drive down to Douglas, and I'll ring Andrew when they arrive."

"We'd better see what Andrew thinks of the idea before we get too far along in our planning," Bessie suggested with a smile.

"Let's go and ask him now."

Harry marched across the sand before Bessie could protest. She rushed to keep up with him. Andrew opened the door with his phone to his ear. He held up a finger and then motioned for them to enter the cottage.

"That's great. I'll talk to you tomorrow, then," he said before pushing a button on the device and dropping it into his pocket. "Hello?" he said quizzically.

Harry looked at Bessie. "Do you want to explain?"

She nodded. "Maggie thinks that Delores and Frank, er, Francis, will be at the Swine and Swallow tonight. I was considering going there to try to talk to Delores, but Harry suggested that we could go into Douglas and see if Hazel is at home while he and Charles go to the pub and keep an eye on Delores and Frank."

"That's a very good idea," Andrew said.

"Can I help?" Matt asked as he came into the room. He

flushed. "Sorry, I wasn't intentionally eavesdropping. I was just coming to find out if anyone had any plans for dinner."

"Dinner sounds good," Andrew said, glancing at his watch. "Do we have any idea when Delores and Frank are due at the pub?"

"Apparently, they go for Quiz Night, which starts at seven, but Maggie said they would probably go earlier," Bessie replied.

"So we should probably head to Douglas now," Andrew suggested. "We could get dinner at the café near Hazel's house while we wait for Harry to let us know that Francis and Delores are in Ramsey."

Bessie nodded. "Give me five minutes to get ready."

"What about me?" Matt asked.

"You're welcome to join either party," Andrew told him. "It all depends on whether you'd rather sit in the pub or go to Douglas and knock on someone's door."

Matt seemed to think for a moment. "I think I'd rather go to Douglas, actually. Pubs have lost a lot of their appeal since I quit drinking."

"I'll just ring Charles and see if he wants to come along," Harry said, pulling out his mobile phone.

Bessie walked towards the door while Harry had a quick conversation with Charles.

"He's on his way," Harry told them a moment later.

"What will you do for dinner?" Bessie asked. "Does the pub do food?"

Harry laughed. "I'd prefer not to eat anything from their kitchens. We'll get something somewhere later."

Bessie frowned. "I don't want you going hungry on my account."

"We'll be fine. Let's see if we can find your friend. That's the most important thing right now."

Bessie wanted to argue further, but she was too worried about Hazel to do so. Instead, she turned and left, heading back to her cottage. Five minutes later, she locked her door behind herself and then began to walk back towards Andrew's cottage.

Harry, Charles, Andrew, and Matt all walked out of the cottage as she approached.

"Is everyone ready?" Andrew asked.

"Yes," Harry said. "We'll ring you as soon as we arrive at the pub."

"I've never been to the Swine and Swallow," Charles said. "It sounds as if it's going to be a very interesting evening."

"Do yourselves a favour and don't win the quiz," Andrew said.

Charles laughed. "It's been years since I did undercover work, but I still remember the basics. We won't do anything that might draw any attention."

"We'll sit quietly and have a few drinks. If we have to take part in the quiz, we'll play as dumb as we can without making ourselves targets," Harry said as he and Charles climbed into a hire car.

"Maybe we should have John or Hugh meet them there," Bessie said.

"They'll be fine. I've no doubt they'll be able to take care of themselves," Andrew assured her.

"Did you describe Delores and Frank to them?" Bessie asked.

"I did," Andrew replied, sounding amused.

Bessie blushed. "I'm sorry. You're the experts."

"And you're worried about your friend. We're all worried about your friend," Matt said. "Let's go."

Bessie got into the passenger seat of Andrew's car. Matt climbed into the back while Andrew got behind the wheel.

Before he turned the key, he reached over and patted Bessie's arm.

"It's going to be okay," he said softly.

"I hope so. I hope it's all just a big misunderstanding and that Hazel is absolutely fine."

"We're all hoping for that."

CHAPTER 14

When they arrived in Douglas, Andrew drove slowly down the street in front of Hazel's house.

"It doesn't look as if anyone is at home," Matt said.

"It's impossible to be certain," Andrew replied. "I'm going to park the car. Matt, I want you to go to the door and knock."

"Me?"

"Francis has never seen you before. If he answers the door, ask for Janet and then apologise for bothering him," Andrew told him.

Matt nodded. "I can do that."

Andrew parked on the street on the opposite side of the road from Hazel's house. That gave him and Bessie a good view of Matt as he crossed the road and knocked. After a short while, he knocked again. When no one answered, he turned and looked at Andrew. Andrew waved for him to return to the car.

"Now what?" Bessie asked.

"Now we wait until Harry rings. Once we know that

Francis and Delores are in Ramsey, we'll try again," Andrew told her.

Bessie sat back in her seat and counted slowly from one to one hundred. When she looked at her watch, only thirty seconds had passed. Sighing, she tried again. She was at seventy-seven when a car rolled past them.

"Isn't that Frank's car?" she asked.

Andrew nodded. "Slide down a bit. I'd rather he didn't see you."

Bessie did her best to duck out of sight while still keeping an eye on the car in question. It stopped at the corner and then disappeared to the left.

"Where is he going?" Bessie asked.

"He may be looking for somewhere to park," Andrew said. "The question is, do I pull out to give him a space or not?"

"That guy is leaving," Matt said, pointing at a man who was climbing into a car a few spaces in front of theirs.

As he drove away, Frank came back down the road. Bessie watched closely as Frank pulled his car into the now-vacant space. A moment later, Frank got out from behind the wheel as Delores emerged from the passenger seat.

"They look as if they're arguing," Bessie said in a whisper.

Andrew lowered his window an inch.

"...six times this week. Just stop," Frank said.

"She's my mother," Delores replied. "I worry about her."

Frank laughed. "You know I'm taking very good care of her."

Delores shrugged. "She's always tired and grumpy these days."

"Is that really something new? When we met, all you did was complain about the woman."

"That doesn't mean I don't love her."

"But you love her money more," Frank said. "We both love her money."

"That's a horrible thing to say."

"The truth can be painful to hear. But that's enough. Let's get her inside and then we can get to the pub."

Delores looked as if she might argue, but then she nodded and opened the rear door to the car. "Come on," she said loudly.

Bessie gasped as Hazel slowly emerged from the back of the car. She looked exhausted and confused as Delores more or less dragged her from the car to her front door. Frank was already there, using a key to open the door for them.

"I take it that's Hazel," Andrew said.

"Yes, and she looked ghastly," Bessie replied. "They must be giving her drugs to keep her quiet and cooperative."

"That would be my guess," Andrew said.

"We need an ambulance," Bessie said. "And the police. They need to arrest Frank and Delores immediately."

Andrew nodded. "I'll ring Pete and see how he wants to deal with this."

As Andrew pulled out his mobile, Hazel's front door opened again. Bessie watched as Frank and Delores walked back to his car.

"We'd better hurry. We don't want to miss the first round," Frank said.

"Yeah, because those are the easy questions," Delores agreed.

They drove away while Andrew was talking to someone at the police station.

"What now?" Bessie asked as Andrew put his phone away.

"Pete is on his way."

"I'm going to knock," Bessie said, reaching for the door handle. "Maybe Hazel will answer."

"She didn't look capable of doing much of anything," Andrew said.

Bessie frowned and then got out of the car. Andrew and Matt followed her to the door. She knocked loudly.

"What would happen if I tried the door, and it was unlocked?" she asked Andrew.

"Opening the door and shouting 'hello' to your friend would probably be okay," Andrew replied.

Bessie nodded and then tried the door. "It's locked."

"Maybe not," Matt said.

He glanced at his father and then pulled a small black pouch out of his pocket. Bessie watched, fascinated, as he pulled several tools out of the pouch. Andrew looked up and down the street as Matt put the tools into the lock and twisted and turned them. A moment later, he opened the door an inch.

"Did you just pick the lock?" Bessie asked.

Matt shrugged. "Dad's friends used to enjoy teaching me different skills."

Andrew sighed. "Nate was not my friend. He was a source, and he shouldn't have been teaching anyone how to pick locks."

"It's a useful life skill. I've never had to worry about forgetting my keys," Matt argued.

Bessie pushed the door open another inch and then shouted, "Hello!" as loudly as she could. After a short silence, she tried again.

"Did you hear something?" Andrew asked after a moment.

"I think so," Bessie said.

"Someone called out for help," Matt said. "I heard it quite distinctly."

"Hello?" Bessie yelled again.

This time they all clearly heard the faint "help" that came from somewhere inside the house.

"Let us go first," Andrew told Bessie.

She shook her head. "You'll frighten poor Hazel to death. I'll go first."

Before Andrew could reply, she pushed the door open and headed into the house. After a quick walk through the ground floor, she rushed up the stairs, calling Hazel's name as she went. She found the woman in bed, her eyes half-closed.

"Hazel? It's Bessie, Bessie Cubbon. Are you okay?"

Hazel opened one eye and then shut them both tightly. "I'm not okay," she said sadly, a single tear sliding down her cheek. "I'm dying."

"Let's get you to Noble's," Bessie said.

"No hospital. They won't help. Frank is helping," Hazel said. "He's good to me."

"I'm glad to hear that." Bessie looked at Andrew.

"Mrs. Lace, I think you should probably see a doctor," he said. "I'm concerned that you may have been drugged."

Hazel opened her eyes and stared at Andrew, clearly struggling to focus on him. "No doctor. No help. Need Frank."

"We can get Frank for you," Bessie said. "Right after a doctor has checked you over thoroughly."

Hazel shook her head and then seemed to drift off to sleep. Bessie anxiously grabbed her wrist to check that she still had a pulse.

"She's asleep. He's probably keeping her sedated so that she's easier to manage," Andrew said. "An ambulance is on the way. Pete should be here any minute, too."

The next hour was a blur for Bessie. Her friend, Douglas CID Inspector Pete Corkill, took a statement from her. She watched as Hazel was taken out of the house on her way to

Noble's, the island's main hospital. When she and Andrew emerged from the house with Matt on their heels, they were greeted by a trio of reporters. Flash bulbs went off in their faces as they tried to walk to Andrew's car.

"What happened in there?" someone shouted.

"It's Bessie. Someone must be dead if Bessie is here," another said.

"Isn't that the inspector from the cold case unit? Maybe they were here to solve a cold case. Maybe Hazel Lace is actually a serial killer, and they finally tracked her down."

Bessie zeroed in on the man who'd made the accusation. "Dan Ross, surely you have better things to do with your time than stand there and make insulting suggestions about a lovely woman. You should be ashamed of yourself."

"Can we quote you on that?" one of the other reporters asked.

Bessie frowned. "No comment," she snapped before she grabbed Andrew's arm and they walked briskly to his car. Matt jumped in as Andrew started the engine.

"Where did they come from?" Bessie asked as Andrew turned the corner.

Andrew shrugged. "I suspect some of the UK papers have sent reporters over to poke around the cold case unit. Hopefully they'll get bored when we all refuse to speak to them."

"As if Dan wasn't enough trouble," Bessie sighed. "Where are we going?"

"I thought we might go to Noble's and check on Hazel," Andrew said. "I'm not certain they'll tell us anything, but we can try."

When they arrived at Noble's, Bessie found an old friend at the information desk. She told them where they could find Hazel.

"We aren't meant to give out that information, but I'll always make an exception for Aunt Bessie," she said.

Bessie and Andrew took the lift to the third floor and then found the private room where Hazel had been put. A uniformed police constable was standing guard outside of the room.

"I'm afraid you can't go in there," he told Bessie firmly. "We aren't allowing anyone to see the patient right now."

Bessie nodded. "Is Pete in there with her?"

"Pete?" he echoed.

"Inspector Peter Corkill," Bessie replied. "We've known one another for a long time now, so I call him Pete."

"I'm afraid I'm not at liberty to reveal the whereabouts of any of our policing team," the man replied.

Bessie nearly laughed out loud. "Of course not."

She pulled out her mobile and found Pete's number. A moment later, everyone could hear a phone ringing loudly.

"Bessie? Where are you?"

"In the corridor outside of Hazel's room."

"I'll be right out," Pete said.

Bessie gave the man a hug when he emerged. "How is she?"

"Confused, mostly. She seems to think that she's dying and that the drugs that Frank keeps giving her are the only thing keeping her alive," Pete replied. "The doctors are running some tests to see what she's been given so that they know what to expect. I'm not going to try questioning her until tomorrow morning."

Bessie sighed. "Does that mean that I can't see her?"

"For now, the doctors want her to sleep. I suggest you come back in the morning, too."

Bessie wanted to argue, but all of the excitement of the evening had caught up to her and she was feeling exhausted.

"What time tomorrow?" Andrew asked.

"I'm going to be here at eight," Pete told him. "I'd prefer to speak to Hazel first, before anyone else."

"We'll be here around nine," Andrew said. "Thank you for all of your help tonight."

Pete nodded. "I just hope that Hazel will become more lucid as the drugs wear off. I'd like to arrest Frank, and maybe Delores as well, but at the moment I don't really have anything with which to charge them."

"Surely they should be in trouble for drugging Hazel," Bessie said.

"That depends on where the drugs came from and whether or not Hazel took them willingly," Pete told her.

"We'll be back in the morning," Andrew said, taking Bessie's arm and leading her away before she could argue any further.

The trio talked about island politics all the way back to Laxey. Bessie knew that Andrew was simply trying to keep her mind off of Hazel, and she was grateful to him for his efforts. When they reached the parking area outside of Bessie's cottage, Charles and Harry were just getting out of Harry's car.

"You didn't even need us in the end," Harry said as Bessie and the others emerged from Andrew's car.

"How was the Swine and Swallow?" Andrew asked.

Harry and Charles exchanged glances.

"Let's just say that we had to work at not winning the pub quiz, mostly because we were the only people in the room who weren't drinking heavily," Charles replied. "After we talked to you and learned that you'd already found Hazel, we may have rung the Ramsey station and let them know that a lot of very drunk people were just about to leave the Swine and Swallow."

"Oh?" Bessie said.

Harry nodded. "Both Frank and Delores ended up getting arrested. They were just walking out of the building when the police arrived. Frank took offense to the idea that the police were stopping people who were drink driving and started shouting at one of the constables."

"That's never a good idea," Matt said.

"When the constable told him to calm down or he might get arrested, he laughed and basically dared the young man to arrest him. As the constable was trying to get Frank into the back of his car, Delores attacked the constable."

"Oh dear," Bessie said.

"When Frank saw what was happening, he jumped into the middle of it all, and it took four constables to break it all up."

"I hope everyone is okay," Matt said.

"The constable who was trying to arrest Frank suffered a few minor injuries. He was lucky that Frank was too drunk to actually land a blow properly. Delores actually did more damage to him, thanks to her long nails," Harry told them.

"So they've both been arrested?" Andrew asked.

"They have. As they were being taken away, Delores said something about having to take care of her ailing mother, but that was all that I heard," Harry replied.

"Hazel is at Noble's," Andrew told him. "She's under police guard. We're going to go back and talk to her in the morning."

Harry nodded. "For what it's worth, I didn't care for Frank or Delores. They were loud and obnoxious for most of the evening."

"And they got nearly every question wrong," Charles added.

The group talked for a short while longer, until Bessie found herself yawning every few minutes.

"I think I need to get some sleep," she said.

Andrew nodded. "We all need sleep. I'll collect you at half eight, and we'll head down to Noble's and see if Hazel is ready to talk to you."

"I just hope she's going to be okay. If she's angry with me for breaking into her house, then she can be angry with me. At least I know I've done everything I can for her."

Andrew walked Bessie back to her cottage and quickly walked through it to make certain that it had been undisturbed while she'd been out. Then he gave her a hug and left her alone. As she reached for the phone to silence the ringer, Bessie picked it up and rang Esther. It was late, but Esther deserved to hear what was happening.

Half an hour later, Bessie took herself off to bed. Esther had been relieved to hear that Hazel had been found, but she was concerned about Hazel's seeming dependence on Frank.

"I'm going to go and see her tomorrow," Esther said. "If she's still talking nonsense about Frank, I'll put her to rights."

Bessie crawled into bed and shut her eyes tightly. *Sleep*, she told herself sternly.

∽

It was just before six when Bessie finally gave up and got out of bed. She'd had a restless night, full of worry about Hazel and unsettling dreams about missing toddlers. As she washed her hair, she wished she could wash her unhappy thoughts away as easily. Ignoring the porridge that she thought she ought to eat, Bessie made herself some toast, covering it with butter and a thick layer of strawberry jam. After that small treat, she went out for her morning walk. Andrew was sitting on the rock behind her cottage when she got back.

"Good morning," she said as she approached him.

"Good morning," he replied. "I hope you slept well."

"I didn't, but it doesn't matter."

He nodded. "I didn't, either. Matt and I had a long conversation about whether I should buy a house on the island or not, and I went to bed with far too much on my mind."

"What does Matt think of the idea?"

"He'd rather I didn't. I think he's afraid that I might decide to sell my flat in London and move here on a permanent basis. Having spent some time on the island, he can see why I love it so much, but, obviously, he'd prefer it if I stayed in London, close to everyone in the family."

"And what do you think?"

"I spent all night trying to decide what I think, and I still don't know. House prices are higher here than I'd hoped. Buying something on the island will cost me more than I'd planned, but it would give me a base here, which would be useful while we're having our meetings every month."

"How much longer do you think we'll be having monthly meetings? Are you planning to keep running the unit indefinitely?"

"Not indefinitely, but until further notice, at least. We're doing very good work here. I've no plans to stop in the foreseeable future."

"Maybe you should have Betty keep sending you properties to consider. It's remotely possible that the perfect place might come along."

"Maybe. But that's a problem for another day. Shall we drive into Douglas and see if we can talk to Hazel?"

Bessie nodded. "Give me a few minutes to get ready. I'll meet you at your car."

They arrived at Noble's a few minutes early. Andrew found a parking space and then they sat in the car until it was nearly nine. Bessie found herself walking quickly across the car park, eager to see her friend. They rode the lift in silence. Pete was waiting for them outside Hazel's door.

"How is she?" Bessie asked.

"Confused and upset," he replied. "The drugs are wearing off, and she's not entirely certain what's happened to her."

"I hope you can put Delores and Frank in prison for a long time," Bessie said.

Pete shrugged. "That will depend on whether Hazel wants to press charges or not. At the moment, she's not ready to make any decisions about that."

"Are Frank and Delores still in custody in Ramsey?" Andrew asked.

"I believe so. I don't think they even know that Hazel is here," Pete replied.

Bessie sighed. "They won't be happy when they find out."

"Which is why we still have a constable with Hazel," Pete told her. "Todd is in there, chatting with her and keeping her calm. He lost his grandmother earlier this year, and he's actually happy to have the assignment. We'll have someone with her or outside her door until she's ready to go home."

"Let's hope she stays here for a while, then," Bessie said.

After a few more minutes of conversation, Pete gestured towards the door. "You can go in and talk to her, but don't worry if she doesn't seem to make sense."

Bessie sighed. "I just hope she's stopped believing that Frank was helping her."

Pete nodded. "I spent some time trying to convince her of that, but she's still a bit too confused to fully understand."

"Here goes nothing," Bessie said. She walked to the door and pushed it open. Andrew and Pete followed her into the room.

Hazel was lying on the bed, holding hands with a young, uniformed constable. They were talking in low voices.

"...in school, but I did my best," Hazel said.

The constable nodded. "I didn't do very well in school. I wanted more than anything to get out into the world. I wanted to work and make money. I didn't think I needed all the stuff school was busy trying to teach me."

"Yes, well, it's never too late to go back," Hazel told him, patting his arm. "My Delores went back recently. That's where she met the most wonderful doctor. His name is Frank. He gives me these tablets that make me feel as if I'm floating." She stopped and frowned. "But that's wrong, isn't it?"

The constable flushed. "Oh, look, you have visitors," he said loudly.

Hazel looked up and stared at Bessie. "This is all your fault," she said angrily.

CHAPTER 15

"I'm sorry," Bessie said as she approached the bed. "I was only doing what I thought was best."

Hazel shook her head. "Frank takes good care of me."

"I got worried when your telephone was out of service," Bessie told her.

"There's nothing wrong with my telephone," Hazel insisted.

Bessie pulled out her mobile and held it up. "Ring it yourself," she suggested.

Hazel tapped in the numbers and then frowned at the device. "That's not right."

"You didn't know?"

"No, of course not. But that's Frank's voice. What has he done?"

Bessie looked at Pete. He shrugged. "We'll see what we can find out," he said.

Hazel waved a hand. "I'm certain it must be a misunderstanding."

"I was concerned initially because I saw the listing for your house," Bessie added.

175

Hazel froze. "Listing for my house?"

"Yes, my friend Andrew is considering buying a property on the island. Your house was one of the ones he was taken to see."

"There must be some mistake. My house isn't for sale. I would never sell that house. It's been my home for longer than many people have been alive."

"I thought that," Bessie told her. "Which is why I rang you as soon as I saw the listing. That was when I got that recorded message."

"It all must be a misunderstanding. Perhaps the listing is for a house near mine. You must have misread the address."

"Except we were taken around it by an estate agent," Bessie told her. "It was your house."

Hazel took a deep breath. "I see. I think I need some rest now. Thank you for coming to see me."

Feeling dismissed, Bessie turned and walk out of the room. Andrew and Pete were right behind her.

"That was sad," Andrew said. "It sounds as if Frank had her convinced that he was helping her while he was trying to sell her house out from under her."

"We'll be investigating," Pete promised. "She should be grateful to you for everything you did."

Bessie nodded, but she couldn't help but feel as if she'd done something wrong. Hazel was angry that Bessie had interfered in her life. Bessie knew that she'd done it out of concern for her friend, but she worried that Hazel would never see it that way.

"Let's go into town and do some shopping," Andrew suggested. "Or at least some window shopping. We can get some lunch while we're at it."

A few hours later, they headed to Ramsey for the cold case unit meeting. Andrew timed it so that they would be early, so that he could ring Sherry for updates before the meeting. While he was talking to her, Bessie paced in the corridor outside of the conference room.

"Have you been inside?" Jasper asked when he arrived a short while later.

"Not yet. Andrew needed to ring someone and I didn't want to hear half of the conversation."

"Ah, well, we have a lovely surprise for you today. Last night, Chef and the pastry chef decided to be friends again, so they made you a special selection of treats today."

"Oh?" Bessie hadn't felt hungry enough to eat much lunch, but a selection of treats sounded quite appealing.

"It's all chocolate-based, because, well, just because. They've made you miniature fairy cakes, chocolate truffles, chocolate bread pudding squares, chocolate mousse, and chocolate brownies. I may have forgotten one or two things, actually."

"That's more than enough things," Bessie said. "And it all sounds as if it will be just what I need to improve my mood."

"I'm glad we were here to help," Jasper laughed. He gave Bessie a hug and then left her pacing. The others arrived a short while later. Bessie was telling them all about the promised puddings when Andrew opened the door.

"Ah, there's been a breakthrough," John said.

Andrew laughed. "And people wonder why I don't play poker," he said. "Come on in and get yourselves some puddings. I'm eager to get started."

Five minutes later, they all had plates full of food in front of them. Even Harry had taken a small brownie square and a single truffle. Hugh's plate was full to almost overflowing. Bessie took a bite of a fairy cake while she waited for Andrew to start.

"This will probably be a very short meeting," he said. "We may spend more time eating than talking about the case."

"Krista knows where Michelle and Dazaray are," Doona guessed.

"Not exactly, but she knows where they went," Andrew replied. "Sherry used all of our suggestions to try to get the woman to talk. It was when Sherry told her about how April rarely goes out now because of everything that happened with Michelle that Krista finally admitted that she knew something."

"And what does she know?" Charles demanded as Andrew popped a truffle into his mouth.

"Sorry, but I couldn't resist," Andrew laughed. "She knows that Michelle left voluntarily. She was reluctant to say more, but she was willing to admit that much."

"Does she know why Michelle left?" Bessie asked.

"Apparently she and Luke were having a lot of disagreements about how to raise Dazaray. Luke thought that Michelle was too easy on Dazaray and that the child needed more discipline. Michelle was thinking of ending things with Luke anyway, but then they had a huge fight on that night in July."

Andrew stopped for a sip of tea.

"It's interesting to me that she turned to Krista for help," John said.

"Krista explained that. She and Michelle had grown a lot closer since they'd had their children, but also she barely knew anyone else in Michelle's circle. She was the perfect person to help Michelle get away because no one would have expected her to be the person that Michelle would ring if she needed help."

"So what happened that night?" Charles asked. "I assume you've heard Krista's version of events."

Andrew nodded. "Michelle and Luke had a bad fight. Krista said she never got all the details, but she thought that Luke had smacked Dazaray for something she'd done, which made Michelle furious. When Michelle told Luke that he couldn't treat Dazaray in that way, he just laughed and said something about how things would be different when they started having children. Then he said he'd already been looking into boarding schools where they could send Dazaray to keep her away from their kids."

"What a horrible thing to say," Bessie said.

"Krista said that Michelle was furious and put Dazaray in her pushchair and headed for the door. Apparently, Luke stopped her and told her that she wasn't allowed to go anywhere."

"How scary," Doona said. "What happened next?"

"Dazaray started throwing up," Andrew told her. "I understand she got violently ill, and Luke started screaming about that. Michelle managed to convince him that she needed to take Dazaray home and get her cleaned up. I gather she promised that she'd be right back as soon as she could."

"Poor Dazaray – but at least they got away," Bessie said.

"Once they were back at Michelle's parents' house, Michelle rang Krista and begged her to help. This is the part that Krista didn't want to share, but Sherry managed to persuade her that it was in everyone's best interest if the police knew the entire story. Krista said she collected them ten minutes later and drove them to the airport. Michelle hadn't packed much. Krista gave her every penny she had in her handbag and watched them get on a flight to Paris."

"Paris?" Charles said.

Andrew nodded. "Michelle told Krista that she had a friend somewhere on the continent, but she wouldn't tell her anything more than that. Krista thought it was someone she'd met while she and Dylan had been travelling. She told Krista that the friend would look after her and Dazaray for a few weeks, or even months, while she tried to work out what to do next."

"And Krista never saw Michelle again?" Bessie asked.

"She did not, but she did get a card from her about a year later," Andrew replied. "It had been posted in Paris and it just said thank you. It also contained money to pay Krista back for what she'd given Michelle at the airport."

"It sounds as if Michelle really doesn't want to be found," Doona said.

"Sherry is going to look anyway. She'd like to be able to close the file if she can. I should say that she's not entirely convinced that Krista is telling the truth, but she does have the card that Michelle sent, which seems to prove that the woman was still alive a year after her disappearance. Sherry is looking into having the handwriting analysed, but she's going to look for Michelle first."

"So now what?" Bessie asked.

"Now Sherry reaches out to the police in France to see if they can help. They might find Michelle tomorrow or they might never find her. It will probably be something between those two, but only time will tell."

Bessie frowned. "That's rather unsatisfactory."

"But we've probably solved another case," Harry said. "The card suggests that Michelle was still alive a year after she'd vanished. Okay, she is still missing, but it's a mostly solved case, anyway."

"Unless Krista is lying and she faked the card," Doona said.

"We've moved things forwards, anyway," Harry said.

They talked in circles for another half hour, revisiting everything they knew about the case, before the conversation finally wound down.

"Let's have dinner together tomorrow night to celebrate

another success," Harry suggested as everyone got ready to leave.

"I'd love that," Bessie said.

"Why don't you all come to my cottage?" Andrew said. "Since Helen isn't here and Matt can't cook, I'll just order pizzas or something."

~

THE NEXT NIGHT felt like a muted celebration for something that was finished but hadn't quite turned out the way everyone had hoped. Bessie found herself talking to Harry a great deal. She was rather surprised to find that she very much enjoyed his company. He and Charles were flying back to London the next morning, but Andrew and Matt were staying on the island for another week.

They filled the week with trips around the island's many historical sites and even found time to visit the Wildlife Park. Bessie's phone rang very early in the morning on the day when Andrew was due to leave.

"Hello?"

"Bessie? It's Hazel Lace. I believe I owe you an apology."

"Hazel, it's so good to hear from you. How are you?"

"I'm a stupid old fool, that's how I am."

"I don't believe that for a moment."

Hazel sighed. "I never imagined that my own daughter would conspire against me. They wanted the house, of course. House prices are quite crazy at the moment, and they simply didn't want to wait for me to die. It isn't as if it's going to be all that long, really, but Delores never did have any patience."

"I am sorry."

"It all started out so innocently. I was dumb enough to believe that Delores and the new man in her life were genuinely concerned about my health. They dragged me to different experts. I've learned now that none of them were experts, of course. They were all Frank's friends, pretending to be doctors. When I started feeling quite unwell, Frank was quick to find just the thing that would make me feel better. The police think that Frank was slipping something into my food to make me feel sick so that he could then convince me to take the medicine he offered."

"My goodness, that's horrible."

Hazel sighed. "And I believed every bit of it. I started taking whatever Frank gave me, and I never complained. Of course, I was too tired and unaware to complain, but I didn't realise that. It wasn't until the drugs finally worked their way out of my system that I woke up and realised that I'd missed several months of my life."

"How very sad."

"They put the house on the market, and the police seem to think that they were planning to kill me once it was sold. They were only keeping me alive so that they could get me to sign the sales paperwork when necessary."

"How truly dreadful."

"I'm just grateful to you for stopping them," Hazel said. "They were very clever about most things, but they worried that my friends might ring, and I might notice the messages on the answering machine, so Frank recorded the fake message about the phone being out of service. It was fine the entire time, but no one knew that."

"I wouldn't have worried if I hadn't seen the house listing from the estate agent."

"If they'd been a bit smarter, they'd have listed it with an agent in the UK. They could have sold it to someone from across and no one on the island would have even known it had gone on the market."

"Thank goodness they weren't very smart."

Hazel chuckled. "I always wanted my children to be smarter, but now I'm quite happy that Delores isn't very bright. She claims that she had no idea what Frank was doing, that she truly thought he was helping me, but no one seems to believe her. I know I don't."

The pair chatted for several more minutes before Hazel finally ended the conversation.

"I'm sorry, but I still get tired very easily. I'd very much like to have lunch with you one day next week, though. I'm going to invite Esther as well. You can both catch me up on all of the skeet I missed."

Their plans made, Bessie put the phone down and sat back in her chair. "That ended quite well, really," she said softly.

The knock on the door made her jump. Andrew was grinning widely when she pulled it open.

"They've found Michelle," she guessed.

Andrew laughed. "Is it that obvious?"

"It is, rather."

"I don't have long before my flight, but I thought we could talk while we walk on the beach. I'm going to miss the beach when I'm back in London."

Bessie slipped on her shoes and then followed Andrew out of the house. "Remind me to tell you about my conversation with Hazel," she said after she'd locked her door.

"You've spoken to her recently?"

"I'd only just finished speaking to her when you knocked."

"I'll go first, though, because otherwise I might explode."

Bessie laughed. "I'm going to assume that means it's good news."

"It's very good news, in that Michelle and Dazaray are both fine. Dazaray is now called Danielle, but Michelle didn't change her own name. The police in France didn't have much trouble finding her, really."

"What did she have to say about her disappearance?"

"She hadn't realised that her parents had reported her missing to the police when she left. She told the police that she'd been fighting with them for weeks and had threatened to leave on several occasions, so she simply assumed that they would realise that she'd gone of her own accord."

"But she didn't take anything with her."

"Apparently, she took her handbag and a small suitcase with a few changes of clothes for herself and for her daughter. She did admit that she didn't take much and that her parents might not have noticed that the small bag and a few of their things were missing."

"Why didn't she take more?"

"She was hurrying to get away before Luke came looking for her. She didn't feel safe staying in Dover, and she didn't want to waste time packing. She was also worried that her parents might get home before she got away. Remember that her parents really liked Luke and wanted her to marry him. She told the French police that she didn't think that they'd believe her if she told them what he'd said to her."

"What a shame."

"She also said that her parents probably would have agreed with Luke about disciplining Dazaray more. She said they used to tell her that she was too lenient with the girl all the time."

Bessie sighed. "So she rang a friend and got that friend to help her get away."

"Exactly. She told the police that she didn't ring April because she knew April wouldn't understand. Krista had a child of her own, so she would understand how badly Michelle wanted to get away after the fight with Luke."

"And Krista truly didn't know where she'd gone?"

"Only that she'd flown to France, nothing more. When she took Michelle to the airport, she promised her that she'd never look for her or tell anyone what had happened that night. Michelle isn't angry with Krista for telling, though. As I said, Michelle never knew that she'd been reported missing. I got the impression that she felt quite bad when she heard that her friends and family had been looking for her for the past ten years."

"I'm not certain why she thought they'd all assume she went voluntarily."

Andrew shrugged. "She'd been fighting with her parents and, obviously, she'd just had a huge fight with Luke. She told the police that she was certain he knew that she'd run away, but that he probably didn't want to admit to anyone that he'd been horrible enough to her to make her run."

"I suppose I can understand that. Is she happy in France?"

"Very happy, I gather. She'd made several friends across Europe during her time travelling with Dylan. When she arrived in Paris, she rang one of them, a young man named Hugo. He lived in the French countryside, and he drove to Paris to collect them. Over time, she and Hugo fell in love, got married, and they now have three children together."

"My goodness. How lovely for them."

"Indeed. The police spoke to Hugo as well, and he confirmed everything that Michelle had told them."

"And, meanwhile, Stanley and Jessica have three grandchildren they've never met."

Andrew nodded. "Michelle did tell the police that she'd been considering visiting Dover in the near future. She said she'd never intended to be gone for as long as she has been and that she feels guilty for not talking to her parents for such a long time."

"I hope they'll be happy to see her."

"She gave Sherry permission to tell her parents where she is, and I understand they've spoken on the telephone already. Sherry has not shared her location with Luke, but she has told him that Michelle and Dazaray have been found and are safe."

"I hope she told April the same thing."

"She did, and she said that April was relieved and then angry, which I suppose is to be expected."

Bessie nodded. "I hope she and Michelle can rebuild their friendship. They'd been friends for a very long time before Michelle disappeared."

"What did Hazel have to say?"

Bessie repeated the conversation she'd had with Hazel. When she was finished, Andrew grinned at her.

"I'm so glad we were able to help her," he said.

Bessie nodded. "I can't believe her own daughter was involved in trying to steal her house from her."

"Children can be quite terrible to their parents."

"I hope you aren't referring to Matt," Bessie said with a teasing smile as the pair turned around and headed back towards Bessie's cottage.

Andrew laughed. "It's been quite nice having him here this month. Helen is planning to come again next month, which is probably for the best, but I've really enjoyed Matt's company far more than I'd expected I would."

"That's good to hear. I've enjoyed getting to know him."

"He needed to get away for a while, too. While he's been here, his solicitor has been working on his divorce. I think he made some actual progress, too, which makes a nice change."

"So your son is going home happy. We found my friend Hazel, and the cold case unit solved another case. All in all, it's been a very productive fortnight."

Andrew nodded. "I continue to be amazed by the success of the unit. One of these months we're going to fail. I'm afraid now that we'll all be far more disappointed than we should be when that happens, seeing as we've had so much success so far."

"We can only do our best. A lot of the credit needs to go to you for selecting the right cases."

"You may not feel that way next month."

"Oh? What do you mean?"

"I have a case in mind for next month that is probably never going to be solved," Andrew told her. "It's murder and it's, well, I can't really tell you anything else, not until the next unit meeting."

Bessie frowned. "That isn't fair."

Andrew laughed. "I'm sorry, but it is for the best. I may end up choosing a different case, anyway. This one has been bothering me for months, though, since I first read through the file summary. I initially rejected it as too difficult, but I can't seem to get it out of my mind."

Bessie frowned. "Maybe I don't want to hear all about it."

"You may hear about it next month, or I may choose a different case altogether. For now, we've all of twenty minutes before I have to leave for the airport. Let's talk about something pleasant."

They talked about the weather and about how, in September, Harry and Charles would be back at the Seaview instead of on the beach. A short while later, Bessie hugged both Matt and Andrew and then watched as Andrew drove away, heading to the airport where he'd return his hire car and catch his flight to London. Matt gave her a cheery wave as he climbed into his car before heading to the ferry terminal in Douglas.

"Maybe we should meet in London one month," Bessie said thoughtfully as she pushed her door shut. "It might be nice to visit London again."

THE LAWRENCE FILE

AN AUNT BESSIE COLD CASE MYSTERY

Release date: February 9, 2024

When the cold case unit meets this time, Andrew isn't the least bit optimistic about their chances to solve the case he's chosen for the month. Three people died at a party in London five years earlier and no one knows for certain who the killer was even targeting. The case had been bothering Andrew since he first read about, though, so he has finally decided to let the unit have a look at it.

It isn't long before Bessie is feeling slightly overwhelmed by the stacks of witness statements from the many partygoers. On top of that, an old friend rings because she's concerned that her brother might be missing.

Bessie had to juggle a discreet search for the missing man while reading through over a hundred witness statements, hoping to find something that everyone else has missed. It's the cold case unit's toughest case yet, but Bessie and her friends are determined to find the solution.

A SNEAK PEEK AT THE LAWRENCE FILE

An Aunt Bessie Cold Case Mystery
Release date: February 9, 2024

Please excuse any typos or minor errors. I have not yet completed final edits on this title.

Chapter One

"Bessie?"

Bessie stopped and looked around. The beach was quiet on the cool and windy September morning, but it still took her a moment to spot the person calling her name. When she recognised Pat, waving at her from the doorway at the back of one of the holiday cottages, she waved. He waved back and then beckoned for her to come closer.

"Good morning," he said as she approached.

"Good morning," she replied with a bright smile. "I feel as if I haven't seen you in ages."

The young man flushed. "I went across for my sister's

wedding and then ended up staying for a bit longer than I'd planned. Maggie and Thomas said it was okay, though."

Bessie nodded. Maggie and Thomas Shimmin owned the row of holiday cottages that ran along Laxey Beach. The first cottage wasn't far from Bessie's cottage, Treoghe Bwaane, which had been her home for a great many years.

When Bessie had first met Pat, he'd been homeless and breaking into one of the cottages at night to shelter from the island's cold and rain. Bessie had introduced him to Thomas and Maggie, and they'd given him a job and place to stay. He'd spent several months during the off-season painting the cottages to get them ready for spring. Once tourist season began, he'd continued to stay in one of the cottages, providing on-site management for the business. Bessie knew that Maggie hadn't been pleased when Pat had gone across for the wedding, worrying that he might not come back, but everyone was happy that Pat was having a chance to reconnect with the sister he barely knew.

"Did you have a good time across, then?" Bessie asked.

Pat nodded. "It was awkward at first, but after a while my sister and I really connected. We had a lot of the same experiences in foster care, and we did our best to remember our lives before we lost Mum. I never thought I wanted family. I mean, I can look after myself, so I told myself I didn't need anyone else, but now that I have Peggy in my life, I can't imagine not having her around."

Bessie smiled. "I'm so happy for you, and for Peggy."

He nodded and then looked behind him into the cottage. "She's here, staying here, I mean."

"Really?" Bessie was surprised.

Pat grinned. "When I told Maggie that she and her new husband couldn't really afford a honeymoon, she suggested that they come and stay in one of the cottages for a few days.

A SNEAK PEEK AT THE LAWRENCE FILE

It took them some time to arrange to get off work together, but they finally managed it."

"How lovely for them."

"They'll only be here for a few days."

"What are you going to do when they go home?"

Pat frowned. "I'm going to miss Peggy a lot, but I'm going to stay here. I have a good job and Maggie and Thomas have done a lot for me. I have a job and a place to stay. Maggie has taught me how to drive and I'm going to start taking classes again next week. It would be foolish to give all of that up, especially since Peggy and I can talk on the phone and text whenever we want."

"I think that's very sensible."

Pat chuckled. "I've not been called sensible very often in my life."

"Pat?"

Bessie smiled at the young woman who'd walked into the room behind Pat. She didn't look much older than eighteen, and she was wearing fuzzy pyjamas, covered in a kitten print, and large white furry slippers.

Pat's smile lit up his face. "Bessie, this is my sister, Peggy."

The girl flushed and then looked down at her pyjamas. "I didn't realise we had company," she said. "I'm sorry. I can go and change."

"You don't need to apologise to me," Bessie told her. "I'm just very happy to meet you."

Peggy nodded. "Pat has told me so much about you. Thank you for helping him so very much."

"I didn't do all that much. He's done all the hard work himself."

Peggy smiled proudly. "He's a good person. He just needed someone else to recognise that and give him a chance."

"He's proven himself many times over," Bessie told her.

"I'm going to go and change. I'll be right back," Peggy said.

Pat and Bessie watched her leave the room.

"That was my sister," Pat said with a small laugh. "I guess you got that."

"I did. There's a very strong family resemblance."

He nodded. "She looks so much like our mother. She's beautiful."

"She is, indeed."

Pat shook his head. "But what is this I hear about a cold case unit? I didn't see the article in the local paper before I went away, but it was all that Maggie wanted to talk about when we spoke while I was across."

"I can't really talk about it," Bessie said. "Everything that is public knowledge was in the article in the *Isle of Man Times*."

"I told Peggy all about it. She was very impressed that I actually know some of the people involved."

"I believe you know all of them, especially since some of them have stayed in the cottages here."

"Now that you say that, you're right. I was just thinking about the people I know who live on the island, but I've met everyone in the unit, haven't I?"

"I'm sure you have."

"But the other two police inspectors, they aren't staying in the holiday cottages this month."

Bessie shook her head. "They've gone back to the Seaview. While they both appreciated having entire cottages to themselves, they both decided that they'd rather have the housekeeping services and room service that the Seaview provides."

"I'd probably feel the same way if that was an option," Pat said with a laugh.

"Feel the same way about what?" Peggy asked as she walked back into the room. She was wearing jeans and a sweatshirt, and she'd pulled her hair back into a loose ponytail.

"We were just talking about the police inspectors who are in the cold case unit with Bessie," Pat explained. "They stayed in holiday cottages here for a few months, but now they've gone back to staying at the Seaview, instead."

Peggy looked at Bessie. "Pat showed me the article about the cold case unit. I was surprised when he told me that he knows a few of the people in the unit, but here you are."

Bessie grinned. "Here I am."

"What's it like? The cold case unit, I mean. After all my years in foster care, I tend to try to avoid the police, but you're working with them all the time," Peggy said.

"It's very interesting work, but everything that we do is confidential, which means I can't really talk about it," Bessie replied.

"But you've solved at least a few of the cold cases, right? That must be very satisfying," Pat said.

Bessie nodded. "We've solved some cases." *Every single one of them,* she added to herself. "And it is very satisfying, especially with murder investigations."

"I'm trying to remember what I read," Peggy said. "Pat said that he's talked to the man who started the unit a bunch of times."

"That's because Inspector Cheatham stays in the cottage on the end of the row every time he comes over. He's been staying there longer than I've been working for Thomas and Maggie," Pat explained. "He likes to stay in the cottage nearest to Bessie's."

Peggy nodded. "Pat pointed out which cottage was yours. It doesn't look anything like the others, of course.

A SNEAK PEEK AT THE LAWRENCE FILE

They're all very much the same. Pat said you've lived there for a long time."

"All of my adult life. I bought the cottage when I was eighteen."

"Wow. I can't imagine owning my own home. Hubby and I don't think we'll ever be able to buy a house."

"Houses on the island were considerably less dear in those days," Bessie told her. "And I inherited some money when the man I was planning to marry passed away."

"Oh, that's really sad," Peggy said. "But if you've lived there ever since, does that mean you never got married?"

"I never did. I've always been quite happy on my own."

Peggy grinned. "I felt that way, especially after my unhappy childhood, right up until I met Paul. I just knew, the first time we talked, that we were meant to be together."

"He's a good guy," Pat said.

"Good for you," Bessie said.

"But we were talking about Inspector Cheatham," Peggy remembered. "Pat said that he used to work for Scotland Yard."

Bessie nodded. "Andrew was a homicide inspector."

"And now he's investigating cold cases with you and a few others," Peggy said. "How did that come about? I'm not trying to be rude or anything, but you aren't exactly the sort of person I'd expect to find working on a cold case unit."

"It's a very unusual unit," Bessie agreed. "Although everyone else involved has at least some connection to the police. I suppose I was asked to join because I'd been involved in a great many murder investigations over the last few years. Andrew and I met during a murder investigation."

"Here on the island?" Pat asked.

"No, across. We were at Lakeview Holiday Park when a man was murdered."

"How dreadful. Did you find the body? Is that why you were involved?" Peggy asked.

"No, but the dead man was my friend's husband," Bessie said, trying to work out how best to explain the complicated situation.

Pat frowned. "How terrible for her."

"They were separated and Doona had filed for divorce," Bessie explained. "But he'd arranged for us to visit the park, hoping for a reconciliation."

"I remember reading something about that in the article about the cold case unit," Peggy said. "Didn't your friend, Doona Moore, inherit the park or something like that?"

"She inherited half of the park. She spends a lot of her time helping to manage the park from afar."

"But she's part of the cold case unit, too, isn't she?" Pat asked.

"She is."

"Did she work for the police before she inherited a holiday park, then?" Peggy wondered.

"She was a receptionist at the station in Laxey," Bessie told her. "We met when she first moved to Laxey from the south of the island. Her second marriage had just broken down and she wanted a change of scenery."

"I don't want to be rude, but how old is she?" Peggy asked.

"She's in her forties, somewhere," Bessie replied. "I don't think age is something that anyone should worry about, though."

Peggy nodded. "I couldn't wait to turn eighteen so that I could get out of the care system, but now that I'm out, I don't really care how old I am."

Bessie had stopped worrying about her age once she'd received her free bus pass. She reckoned that she was somewhere in the later part of middle age and she was determined not to give the matter any additional thought until she received a birthday card from the Queen.

"She's very nice," Pat said. "I bump into her all over Laxey. A lot of the time she has one of John Rockwell's kids with her. Sometimes she has both of them."

Bessie nodded. "She does as much as she can to help him with Thomas and Amy."

"I'm lost," Peggy laughed.

"Inspector John Rockwell is another member of the cold case unit," Pat told her. "He's in charge of the police station here in Laxey, but he's from across somewhere. I don't know how long he's been on the island."

"He's been here over three years," Bessie said. "I met him right after he moved across and we've been friends ever since."

"And he has two children?" Peggy asked.

"Yes, Thomas and Amy. Thomas is off to university any day now. He's decided to go to a school in Manchester. That's where the family lived before John took the job on the island," Bessie told her.

Peggy frowned. "Pat said that Doona helps with the children. Is their mother in Manchester?"

Pat shook his head. "I told you about her," he said. "She and Inspector Rockwell got divorced and then she married some doctor who'd been treating her mother. They went to Africa for their honeymoon, and she died under mysterious circumstances."

Peggy looked at Bessie. "Really? Is all of that true?"

"Unfortunately, it is true," Bessie confirmed.

"I didn't think people died under mysterious circumstances in real life," Peggy said. "No one I know has ever died under mysterious circumstances."

"Thankfully, it doesn't happen very often," Bessie said.

"So Inspector Rockwell is part of the cold case unit and he's in charge of the Laxey station and he's raising two kids on his own?" Peggy asked.

"Yes to all of that, but Doona helps when she can," Bessie replied.

Peggy frowned. "How old is Inspector Rockwell? Are he and Doona a couple or is she just being nice?"

"Doona and John have been seeing each other for a while now," Bessie said. "Only they know how serious their relationship is, though."

"Wasn't there a much younger policeman in the unit, too?" Peggy asked.

Pat grinned. "Hugh Watterson. He's just a constable, but he's smart and he's also really nice."

"Didn't you tell me something about his wife?" Peggy asked her brother.

"Yeah, his wife, Grace, does some tutoring at the college. She's only there a few hours each week, because she has a little one, but she was the person who finally got me to understand a little bit of algebra."

"Grace was a primary school teacher before she had Aalish," Bessie added. "I didn't realise she was tutoring at the college, though."

Pat shrugged. "Like I said, she's only there a few hours a week. She said something about how her mother loves having the baby all to herself for a few hours, so she decided to do something useful with the time."

Bessie nodded, wondering if Grace would keep tutoring after baby number two arrived in February, but not voicing her thoughts.

"I'm trying to remember what I read," Peggy said. "Is that all the unit members from the island?"

"It is," Bessie said. "The other two members come across

from London for our meetings. Andrew does, too, of course."

"So who are the other two?" Peggy asked.

"Inspector Harry Blake and Inspector Charles Morris," Bessie told her. "They're both retired from Scotland Yard. Harry was a homicide inspector. Charles was an expert in missing persons."

Pat nodded. "I only talked to Harry once or twice, aside from giving him his keys each time he came over. He wasn't ever rude, but he was always abrupt and never wanted to chat. When his telly broke, he called and told me that it wasn't working, but then said that he didn't want me to come over and repair it until after he'd gone."

Peggy frowned. "Imagine living without a working telly."

Bessie grinned. "I don't have a telly."

Peggy's jaw dropped. "What do you do with your time?"

"I've never had trouble filling my time. I love to read, and I've spent years working as an amateur historian as well. I read and transcribe old documents for the Manx Museum Library. I have friends with whom I enjoy spending time. I like to visit the island's historical sites, and I enjoy shopping trips and going out for meals."

"I wish I liked to read," Peggy said with a sigh. "I'm afraid I find it a chore."

"You need to work out what sorts of books you want to read," Bessie told her. "Once you do that, you'll find you love reading."

"She's right," Pat said. "She's made me love reading and I used to hate it."

"I'd be more than happy to lend you a few books," Bessie said. "Maybe, while you're here, you can start to work out what genres you enjoy."

Pat laughed. "She is on her honeymoon," he said. "Maybe this isn't the best time."

Bessie felt her cheeks redden. "The offer is good whenever you're on the island," she said.

"When the other inspector stayed here, was he friendlier?" Peggy asked Pat.

He shrugged. "A bit, yeah, but there's something sad about him. Inspector Blake has world-weary eyes. Inspector Morris has sad eyes."

"You're very observant," Bessie said, agreeing with Pat's assessment of the two men.

"You learn to be in foster care," Pat said. "I moved around a lot. You learn how to read people for your own protection."

Peggy nodded. "I didn't get moved around as much as Pat, but that's because I learned to keep my mouth shut and keep my head down. Pat was too stubborn for his own good."

Pat shrugged. "I was angry at the world, and I took it out on everyone. I was fortunate that a few people believed in me, regardless."

"And now you know police inspectors and business owners and you're in school, learning things so you can have a better future," Peggy said proudly.

Pat flushed. "And it's all thanks to Aunt Bessie."

She shook her head. "You've worked really hard to get where you are today, and I know you're going to keep working hard and that you're going to accomplish amazing things."

"That's my brother," Peggy said happily.

"I hope you enjoy your stay on the island," Bessie told her.

"I'm sure we will. I know Pat would love for us to move here, but my husband and I both have good jobs back home. We'll just have to visit a lot."

"Maggie and Thomas have said that they're welcome to come and stay any time the cottages aren't fully booked," Pat said. "Which means they can visit pretty much any time of the year, aside from the busiest summer months."

"That was kind of Maggie and Thomas," Bessie said.

"They've been great," Pat said.

"They took us all out for dinner the first night we were here," Peggy said. "I had never eaten at such a fancy restaurant before."

"It was really nice," Pat said.

A buzzing noise made Bessie jump. Pat pulled out his mobile phone.

"Speak of the devil," he said with a grin. "Hello?"

Bessie smiled at Peggy as Pat walked away with the phone pressed to his ear.

"How long are you going to be staying on the island?" she asked the girl.

"Just two more nights. I wish we could stay longer, but Paul and I both need to get back to work. We're already planning for a big family Christmas here, though. I'm trying to find our older sister. Pat and I would both love to see her again."

"That would be nice."

"I'm not sure she wants to be found," Peggy said softly. "She told me once that once she got out of the system, she was going to disappear and start a whole new life where no one knew her or knew anything about her past. I don't blame her for feeling that way, but I miss her."

"If you need any help finding her, I may know someone who can help."

Peggy grinned. "I'm not sure we should have a bunch of Scotland Yard inspectors looking for her, but I may ask for your help anyway. I have a few friends to talk to first, though, people who were in the system with her. I think we'll be able to track her down."

"Good luck."

A SNEAK PEEK AT THE LAWRENCE FILE

"That was Maggie," Pat said as he walked back across the room. He stuck his phone in his pocket and then shrugged. "Thomas isn't feeling well this morning, so Maggie isn't going to be able to come down and help with today's departures and arrivals. She suggested that you might be willing to help," he told Peggy.

She looked surprised. "Help with your work?"

Pat nodded. "She said she'll pay you for your time, and that you don't have to if you don't want to, but if we get several guests departing and others arriving at the same time, I might need some help."

"Is that likely?" Peggy asked.

Pat laughed. "We have two guests leaving today and three guests arriving today. The departures are all supposed to happen before eleven, and the new arrivals can arrive at any time after midday and before midnight. It seems unlikely that anyone will overlap, but I suppose it's possible."

Peggy glanced at the watch. "It's only half seven. I can probably be presentable in an hour or so if you want me to help."

"You can sit in the office with me this afternoon, anyway," Pat suggested. "I'll get the cleaning done in the two cottages with departures and then we just have to wait for the new arrivals. You and Paul didn't have plans for today, did you?"

"My plans for the visit are just to spend as much time with you as possible."

Pat nodded. "Next time they come over, we'll have you suggest some sights they should see," he told Bessie.

"I'd be happy to do that," Bessie told him. "But for now, I should get back to my walk."

Peggy gave her a quick hug before Pat gave her a longer one.

"It was nice meeting you," Peggy said.

"Likewise. I hope you enjoy your stay," Bessie replied.

A SNEAK PEEK AT THE LAWRENCE FILE

She walked back down the sand towards the water. Before she began walking again, she looked back and waved at the brother and sister who were standing at the back of the cottage, watching her. They both waved before they shut the sliding door and disappeared from view.

ALSO BY DIANA XARISSA

The Aunt Bessie Cold Case Mysteries

The Adams File
The Bernhard File
The Carter File
The Durand File
The Evans File
The Flowers File
The Goodman File
The Howard File
The Irving File
The Jordan File
The Keller File
The Lawrence File

The Isle of Man Cozy Mysteries

Aunt Bessie Assumes
Aunt Bessie Believes
Aunt Bessie Considers
Aunt Bessie Decides
Aunt Bessie Enjoys
Aunt Bessie Finds
Aunt Bessie Goes
Aunt Bessie's Holiday
Aunt Bessie Invites

Aunt Bessie Joins

Aunt Bessie Knows

Aunt Bessie Likes

Aunt Bessie Meets

Aunt Bessie Needs

Aunt Bessie Observes

Aunt Bessie Provides

Aunt Bessie Questions

Aunt Bessie Remembers

Aunt Bessie Solves

Aunt Bessie Tries

Aunt Bessie Understands

Aunt Bessie Volunteers

Aunt Bessie Wonders

Aunt Bessie's X-Ray

Aunt Bessie Yearns

Aunt Bessie Zeroes In

The Isle of Man Ghostly Cozy Mysteries

Arrivals and Arrests

Boats and Bad Guys

Cars and Cold Cases

Dogs and Danger

Encounters and Enemies

Friends and Frauds

Guests and Guilt

Hop-tu-Naa and Homicide

Invitations and Investigations

Joy and Jealousy

Kittens and Killers

Letters and Lawsuits

Marsupials and Murder

Neighbors and Nightmares

Orchestras and Obsessions

Proposals and Poison

Questions and Quarrels

Roses and Revenge

Secrets and Suspects

Theaters and Threats

Umbrellas and Undertakers

Visitors and Victims

Weddings and Witnesses

Xylophones and X-Rays

Yachts and Yelps

Zephyrs and Zombies

The Markham Sisters Cozy Mystery Novellas

The Appleton Case

The Bennett Case

The Chalmers Case

The Donaldson Case

The Ellsworth Case

The Fenton Case

The Green Case

The Hampton Case

The Irwin Case

The Jackson Case
The Kingston Case
The Lawley Case
The Moody Case
The Norman Case
The Osborne Case
The Patrone Case
The Quinton Case
The Rhodes Case
The Somerset Case
The Tanner Case
The Underwood Case
The Vernon Case
The Walters Case
The Xanders Case
The Young Case
The Zachery Case

The Janet Markham Bennett Cozy Thrillers

The Armstrong Assignment
The Blake Assignment
The Carlson Assignment
The Doyle Assignment
The Everest Assignment
The Farnsley Assignment
The George Assignment
The Hamilton Assignment
The Ingram Assignment

The Jacobs Assignment
The Knox Assignment

The Sunset Lodge Mysteries

The Body in the Annex
The Body in the Boathouse
The Body in the Cottage
The Body in the Dunk Tank
The Body in the Elevator

The Lady Elizabeth Cozies in Space

Alibis in Alpha Sector
Bodies in Beta Sector
Corpses in Chaos Sector
Danger in Delta Sector

The Midlife Crisis Mysteries

Anxious in Nevada
Bewildered in Florida
Confused in Pennsylvania
Dazed in Colorado

The Isle of Man Romances

Island Escape
Island Inheritance
Island Heritage
Island Christmas

The Later in Life Love Stories

Second Chances
Second Act
Second Thoughts
Second Degree
Second Best
Second Nature
Second Place
Second Dance

BOOKPLATES ARE NOW AVAILABLE

Would you like a signed bookplate for this book?

I now have bookplates (stickers) that I can personalize, sign, and send to you. It's the next best thing to getting a signed copy!

Send an email to diana@dianaxarissa.com with your mailing address (I promise not to use it for anything else, ever) and how you'd like your bookplate personalized and I'll sign one and send it to you.

There is no charge for a bookplate, but there is a limit of one per person.

ABOUT THE AUTHOR

Diana has been self-publishing since 2013, and she feels surprised and delighted to have found readers who enjoy the stories and characters that she imagines. Always an avid reader, she still loves nothing more than getting lost in fictional worlds, her own or others!

After being raised in Erie, Pennsylvania, and studying history at Allegheny College in Meadville, Pennsylvania, Diana pursued a career in college administration. She was living and working in Washington, DC, when she met her future husband, an Englishman who was visiting the city.

Following her marriage, Diana moved to Derbyshire. A short while later, she and her husband relocated to the Isle of Man. After ten years on the island, during which Diana earned a Master's degree in the island's history, they made the decision to relocate again, this time to the US.

Now living near Buffalo, New York, Diana and her husband live with their daughter, a student at the University at Buffalo. Their son is now living and working just outside of Boston, Massachusetts, giving Diana an excuse to travel now and again.

Diana also writes mystery/thrillers set in the not-too-distant future as Diana X. Dunn and Young Adult fiction as D.X. Dunn.

She is always happy to hear from readers. You can write to her at:

Diana Xarissa Dunn
PO Box 72
Clarence, NY 14031.

Find Diana at: DianaXarissa.com
E-mail: Diana@dianaxarissa.com

Made in the USA
Columbia, SC
18 May 2024